W9-AUY-295

THE INVINCIBLE IRON MAN™

AN ORIGIN STORY

Based on the Marvel comic book series **The Invincible Iron Man**

Adapted by Rich Thomas

Interior Illustrated by Craig Rousseau *and* Hi-Fi Design

New York

visit us at www.abdopublishing.com

Reinforced library bound edition published in 2013 by Spotlight, a division of the ABDO Group, PO Box 398166, Minneapolis, MN 55439. Spotlight produces high-quality reinforced library bound editions for schools and libraries. Published by agreement with Marvel Press, an imprint of Disney Book Group, LLC.

Printed in the United States of America, North Mankato, Minnesota.
042012
052013
♻ This book contains at least 10% recycled materials.

TM & © 2012 Marvel & Subs.

No part of this book may be reproduced or transmitted in any form or by any means, electronic or mechanical, including photocopying, recording, or by any information storage and retrieval system, without written permission from the publisher.

Library of Congress Cataloging-in-Publication Data

This book was previously cataloged with the following information:
Thomas, Richard.
The invincible Iron Man origin storybook / [edited by] Nachie Castro.
p. cm.
1. Iron Man (Fictitious character)—Juvenile fiction. 2. Superheroes—Juvenile fiction. I. Title.
PZ7.T36933 2012
[E]-dc223

2010938847

ISBN 978-1-61479-010-5 (reinforced library edition)

All Spotlight books are reinforced library binding and manufactured in the United States of America.

DEC -- 2013

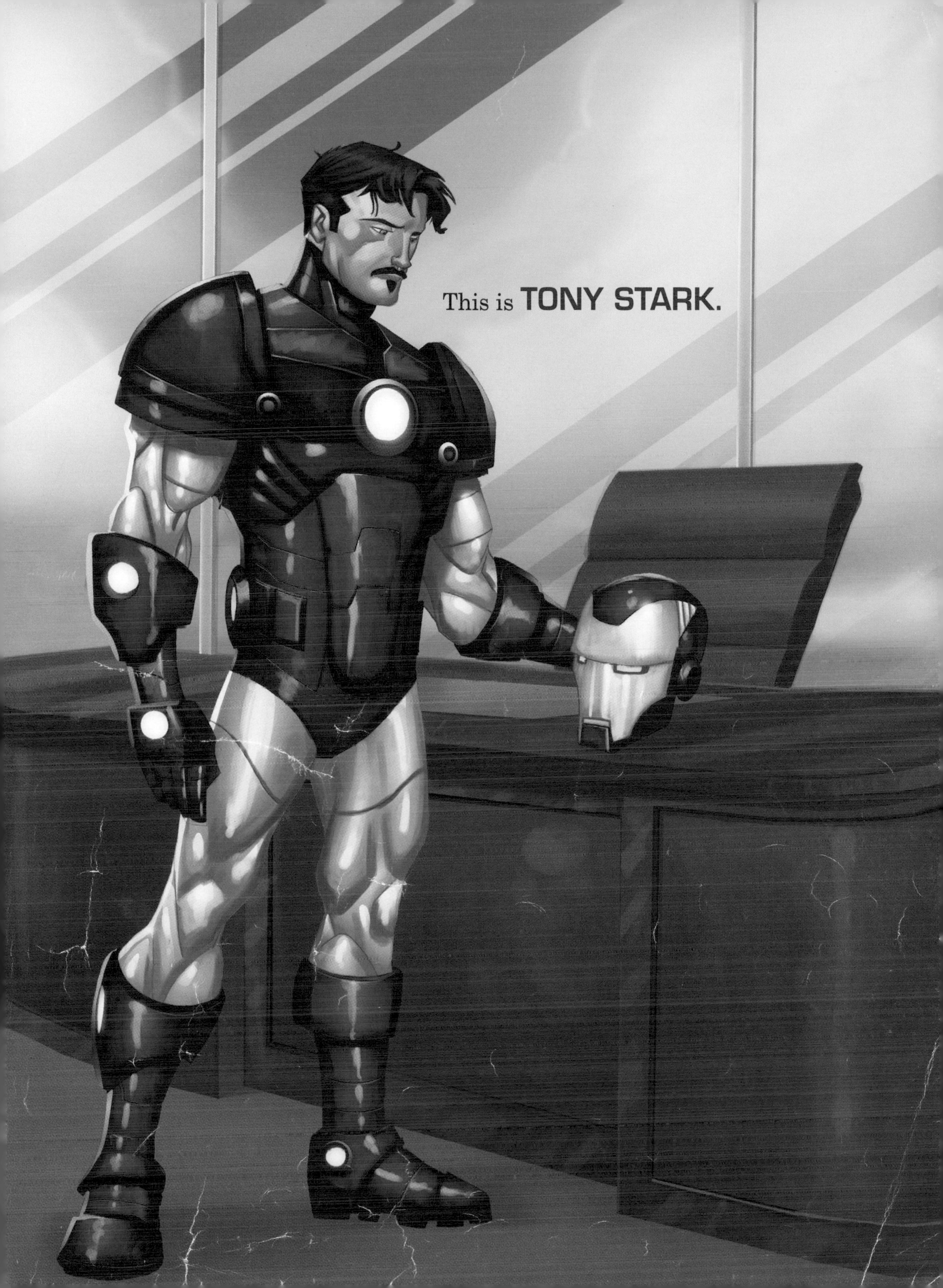

This is **TONY STARK.**

Tony is usually as regular a guy as you or me
—but with **a lot more money.**

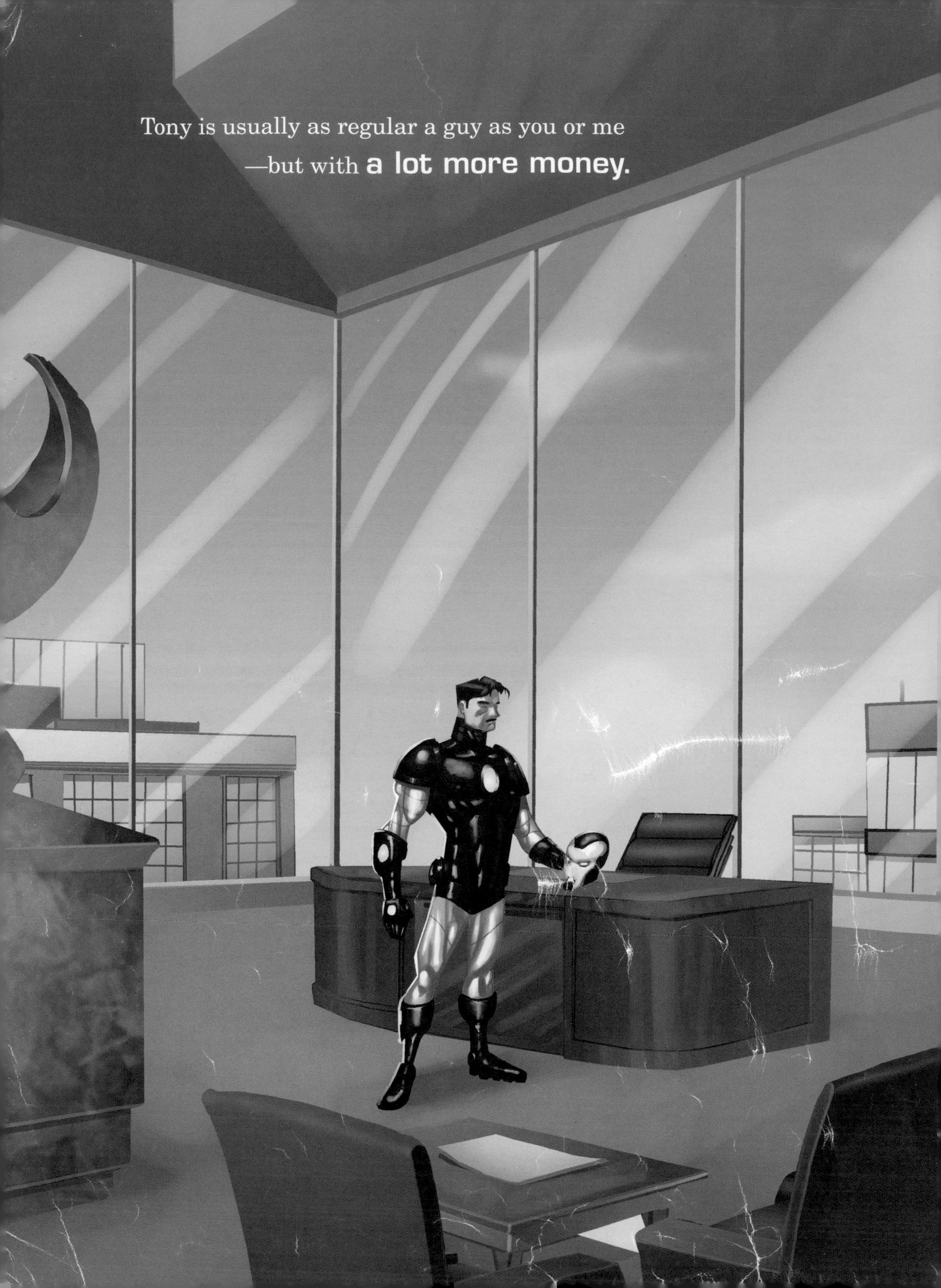

When Tony puts on his special armor, he becomes more **powerful** than most people.

He even calls himself something different—

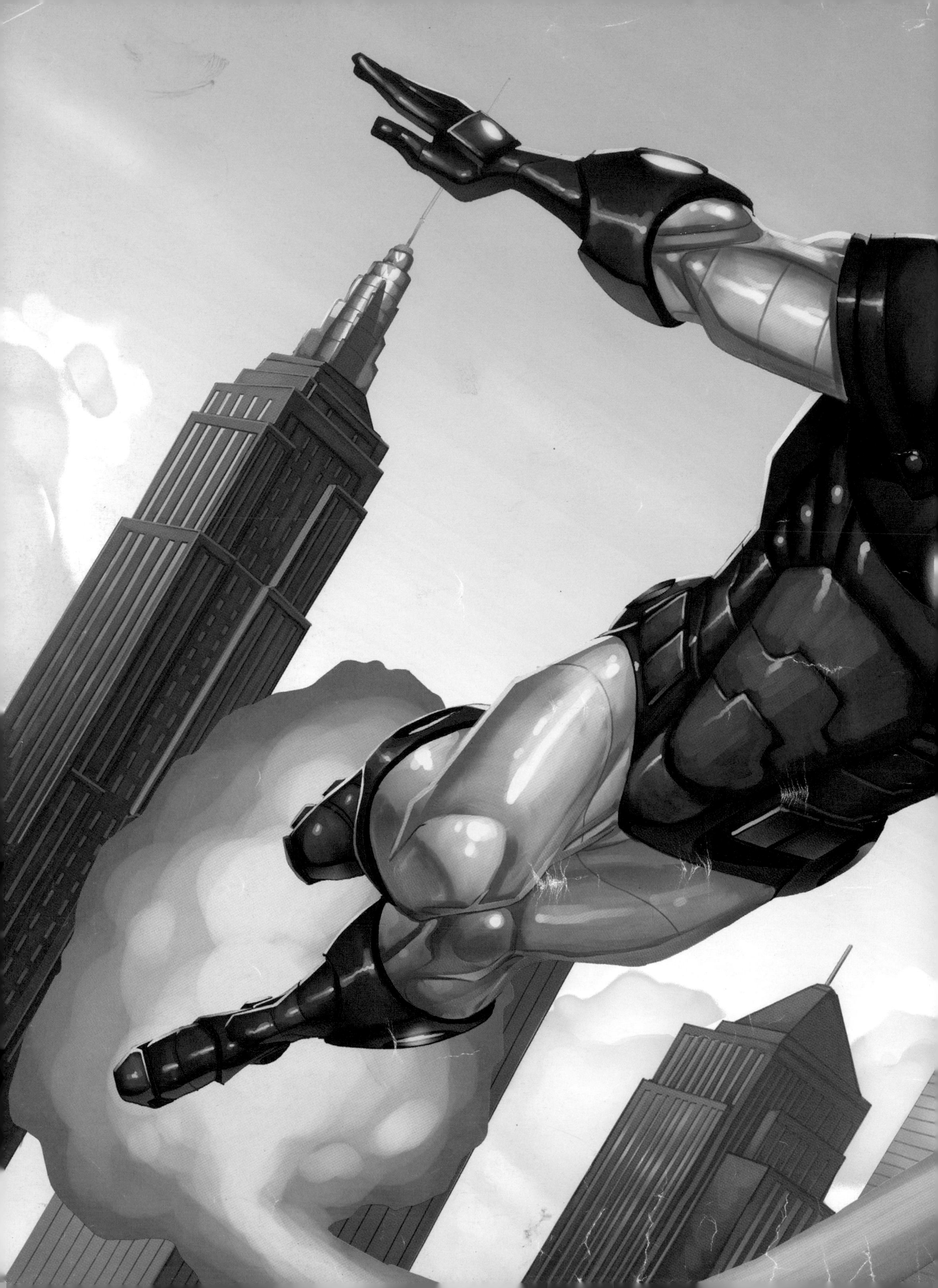

THE INVINCIBLE IRON MAN!

But Tony wasn't born a Super Hero.

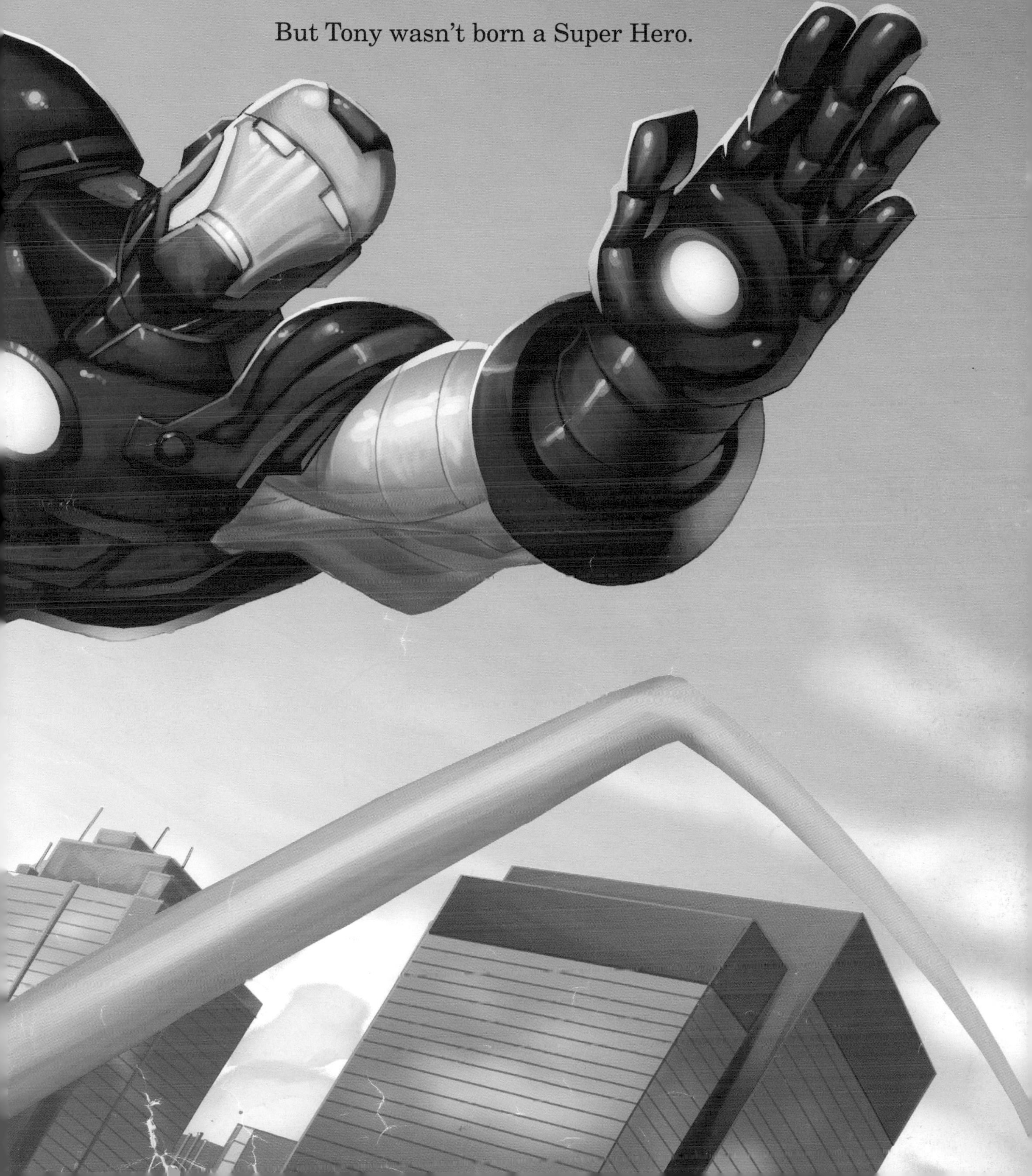

He hasn't always fought
to **protect** people.

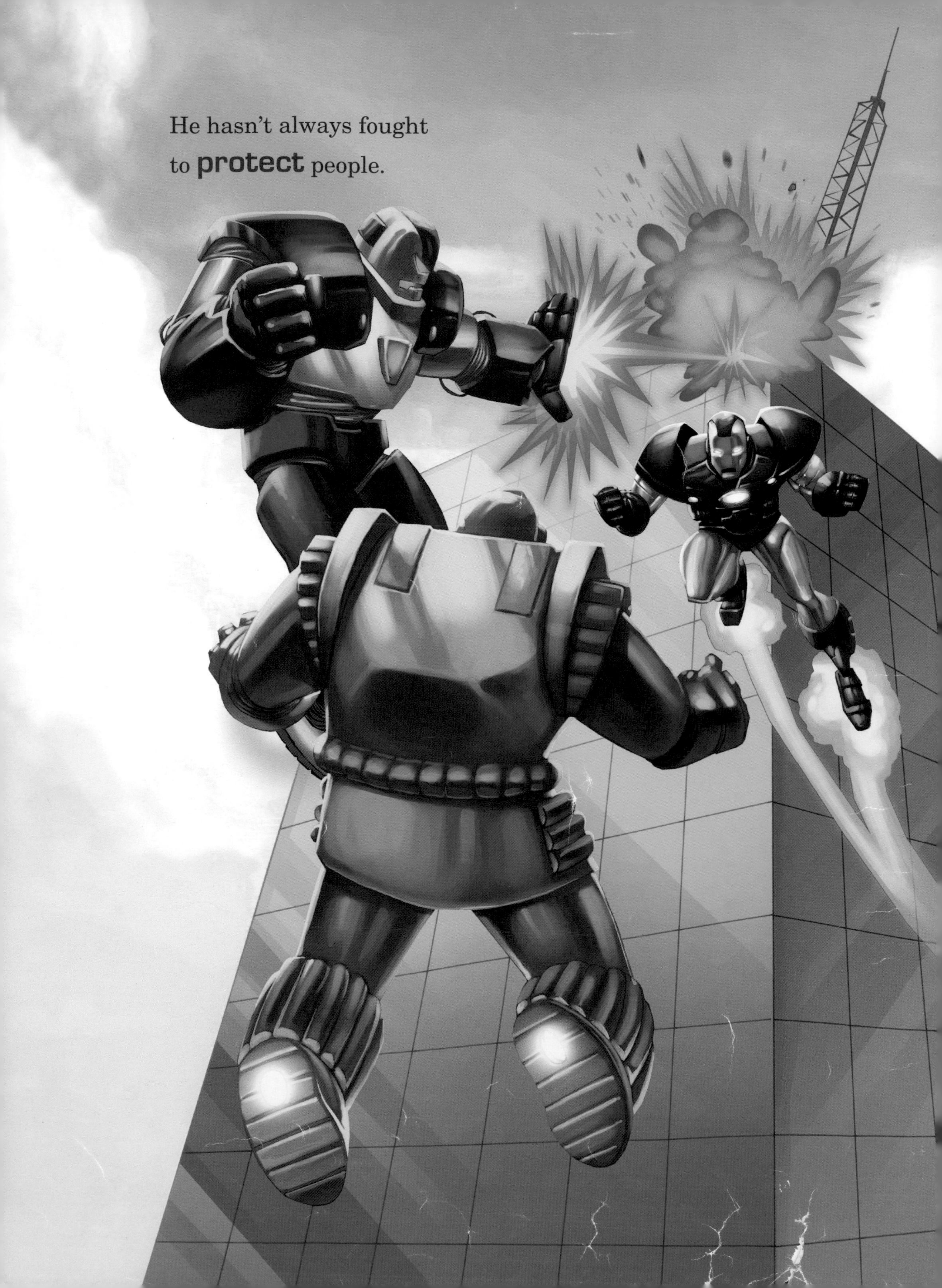

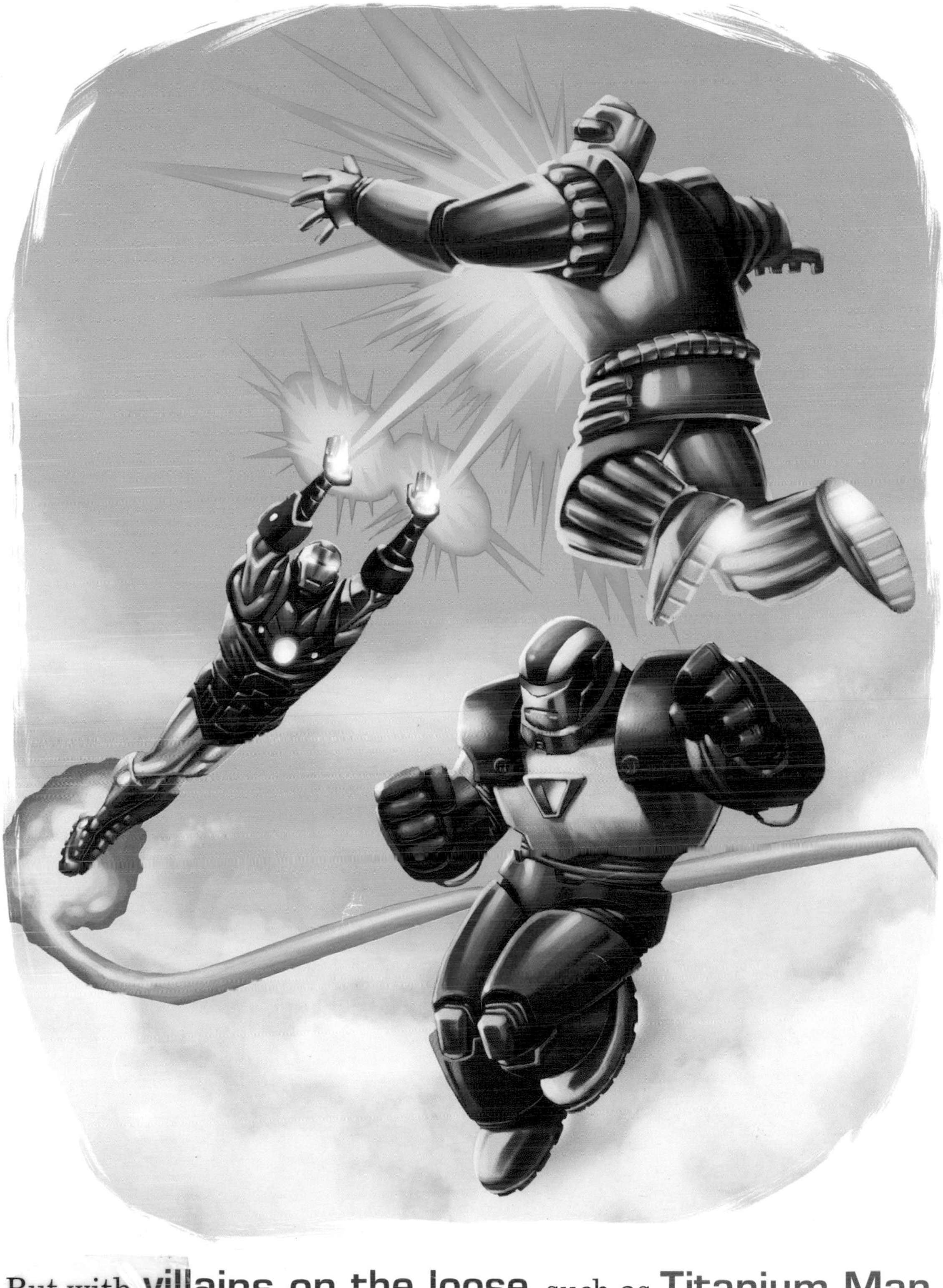

But with **villains on the loose**, such as **Titanium Man** and **Iron Monger**—who both use Tony's technology for their own evil purposes—

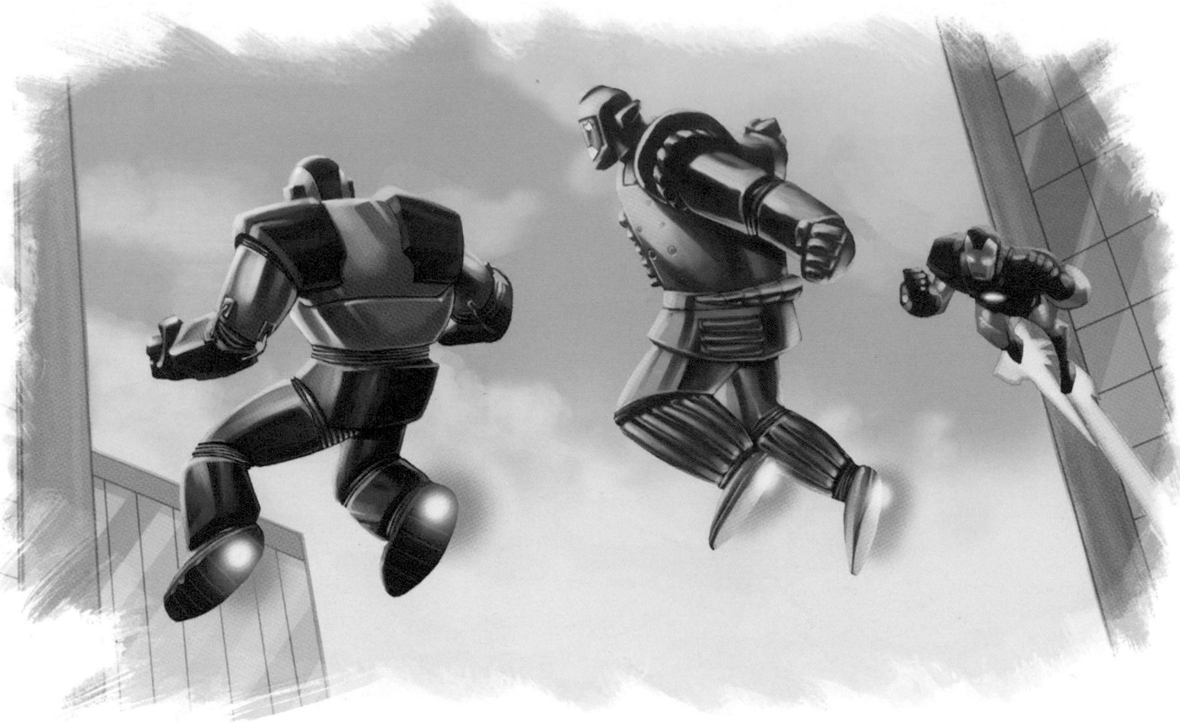

Tony feels it's his responsibility to stop them!

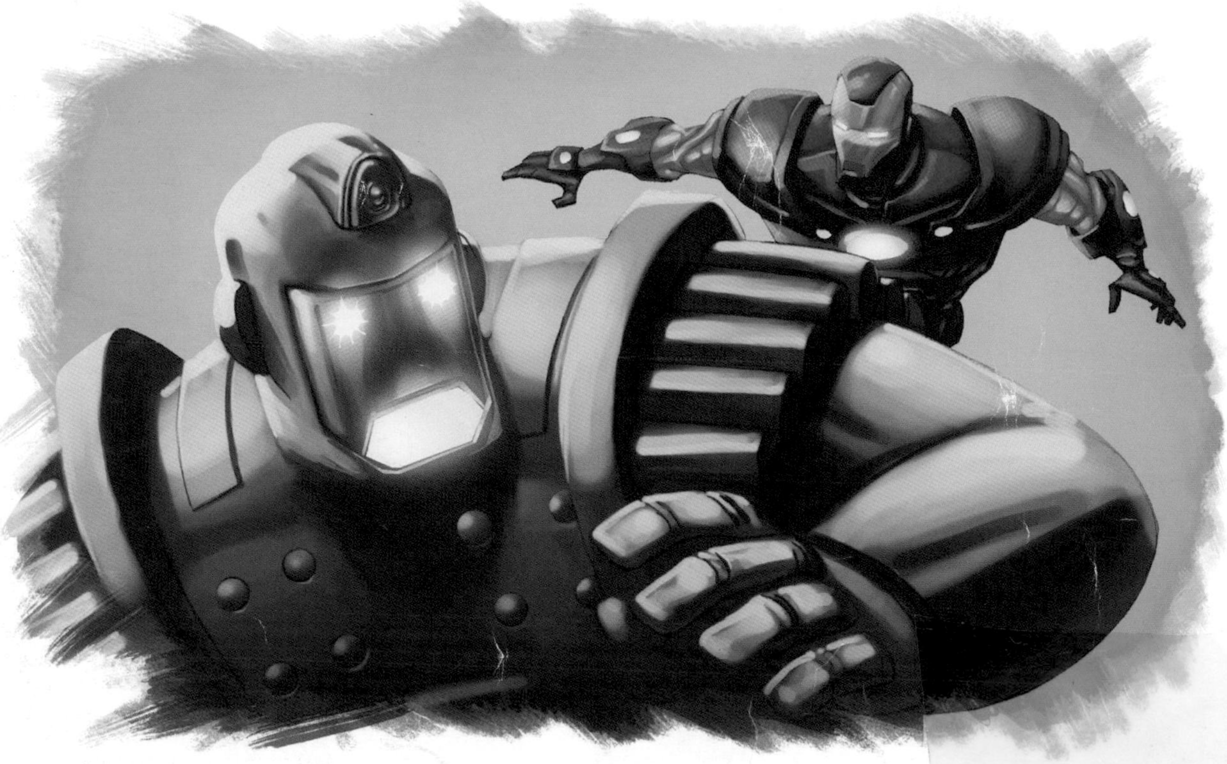

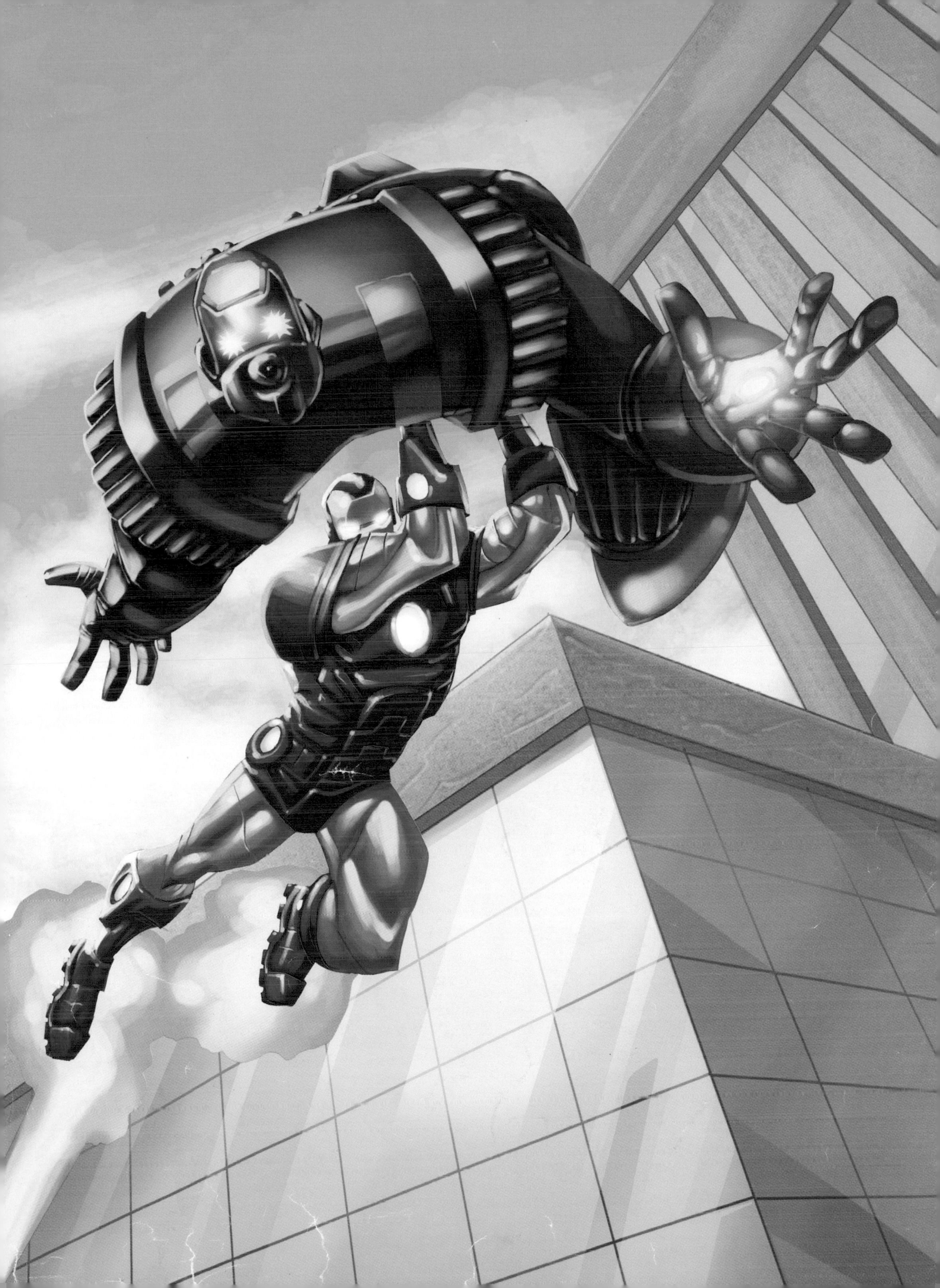

Tony didn't always get the job done this easily.

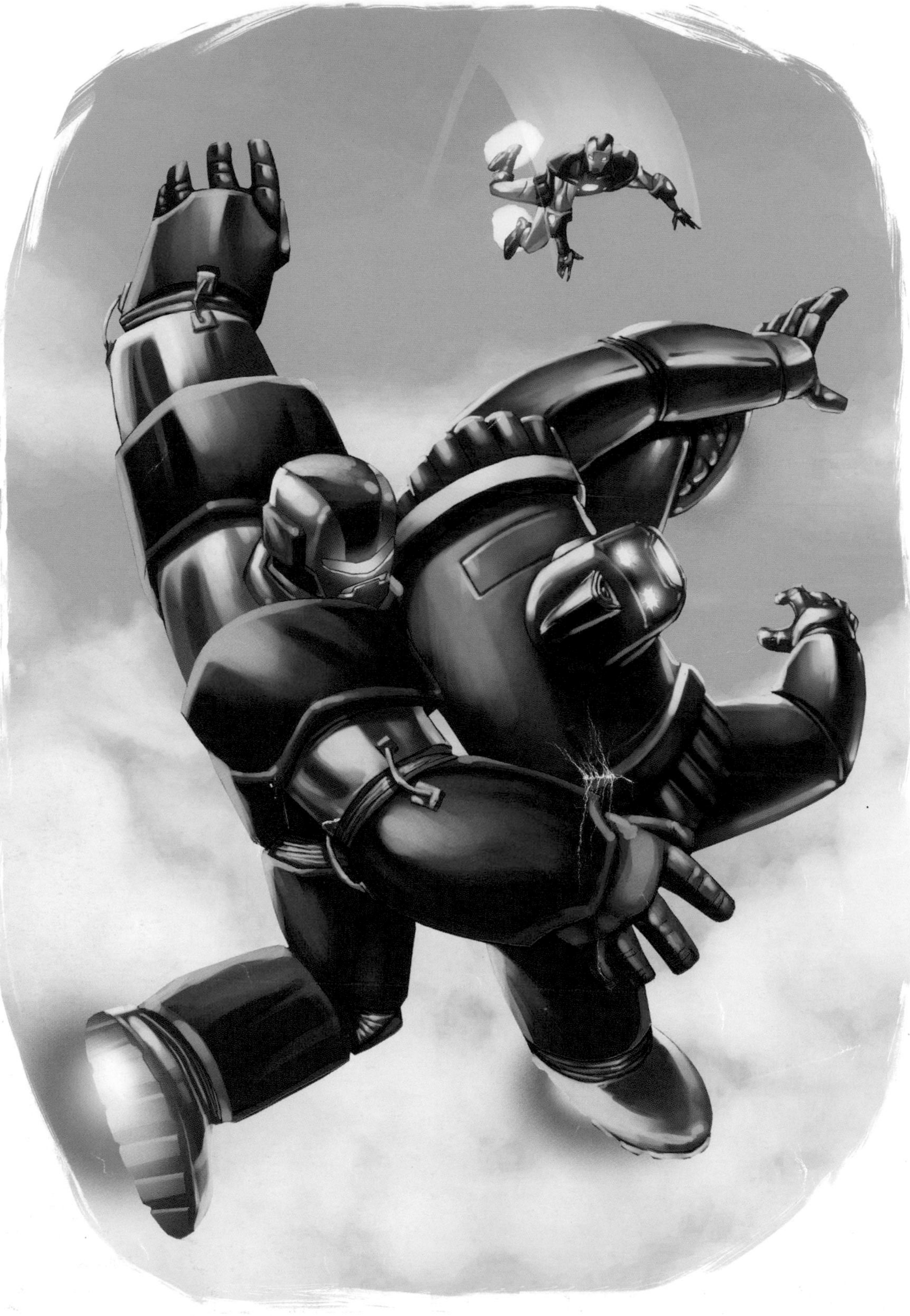

Or this well.

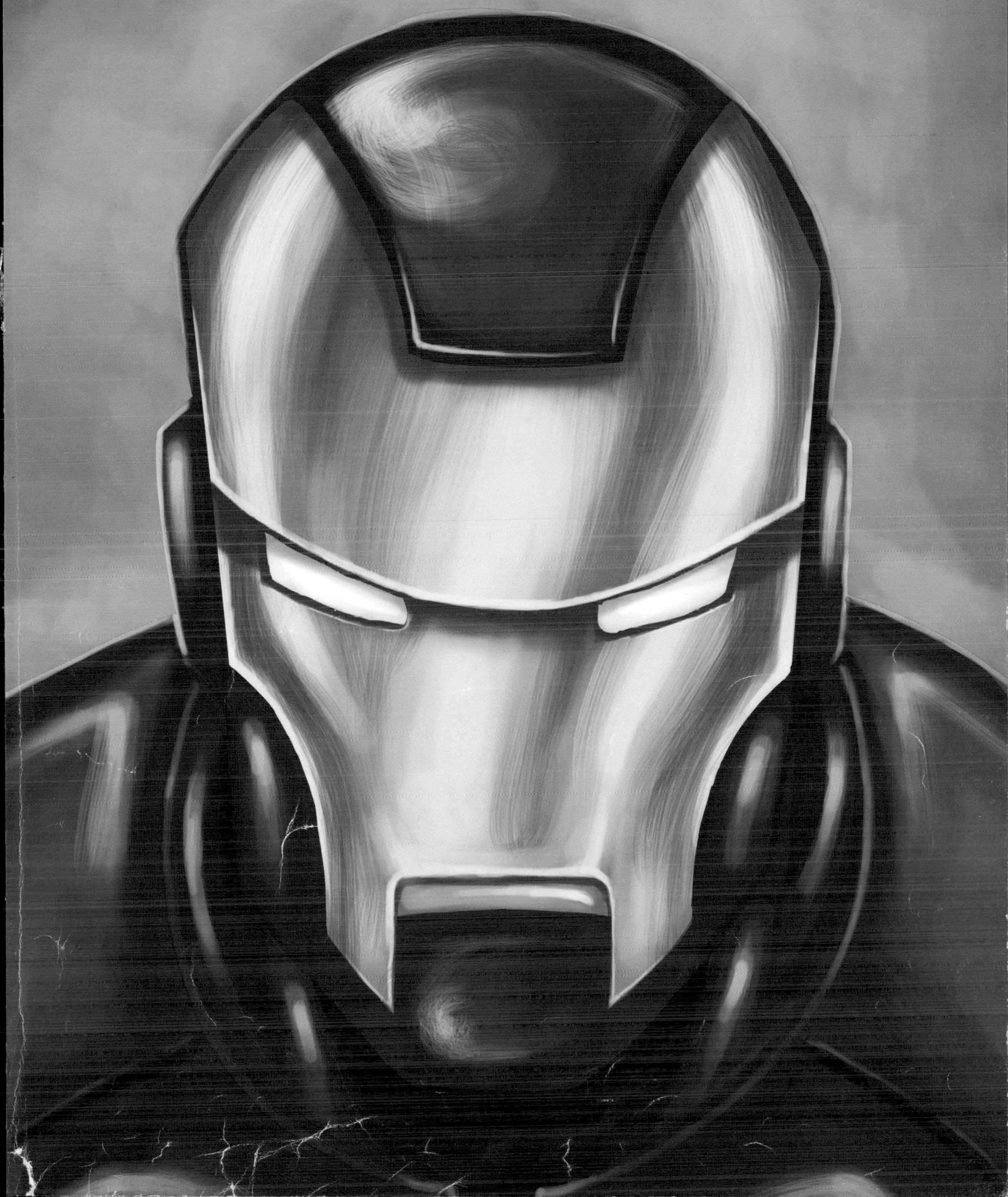

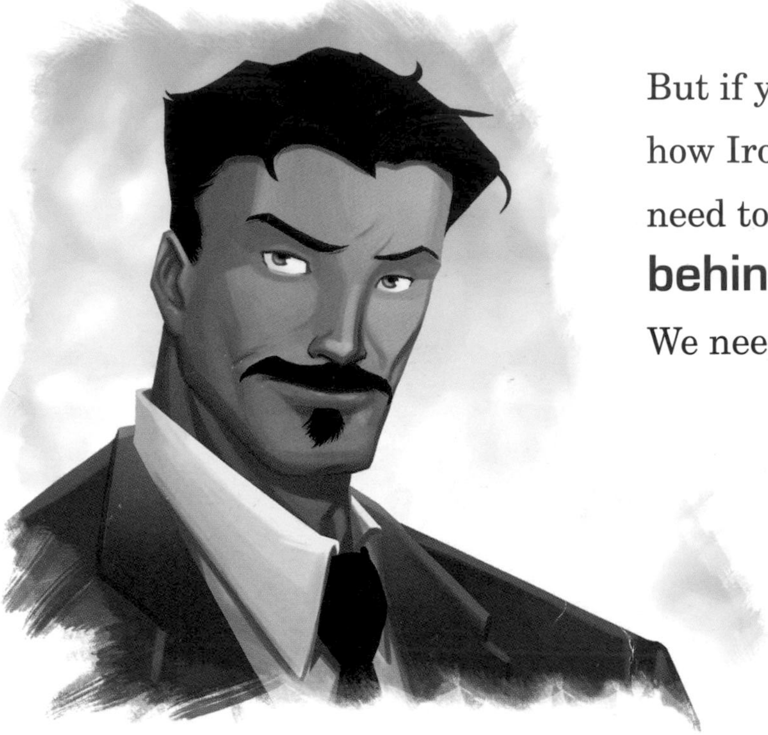

But if you really want to know how Iron Man was born, we need to start with the **man behind the mask.** We need to start with **Tony.**

Tony had so much money that he could **go anywhere** he wanted.

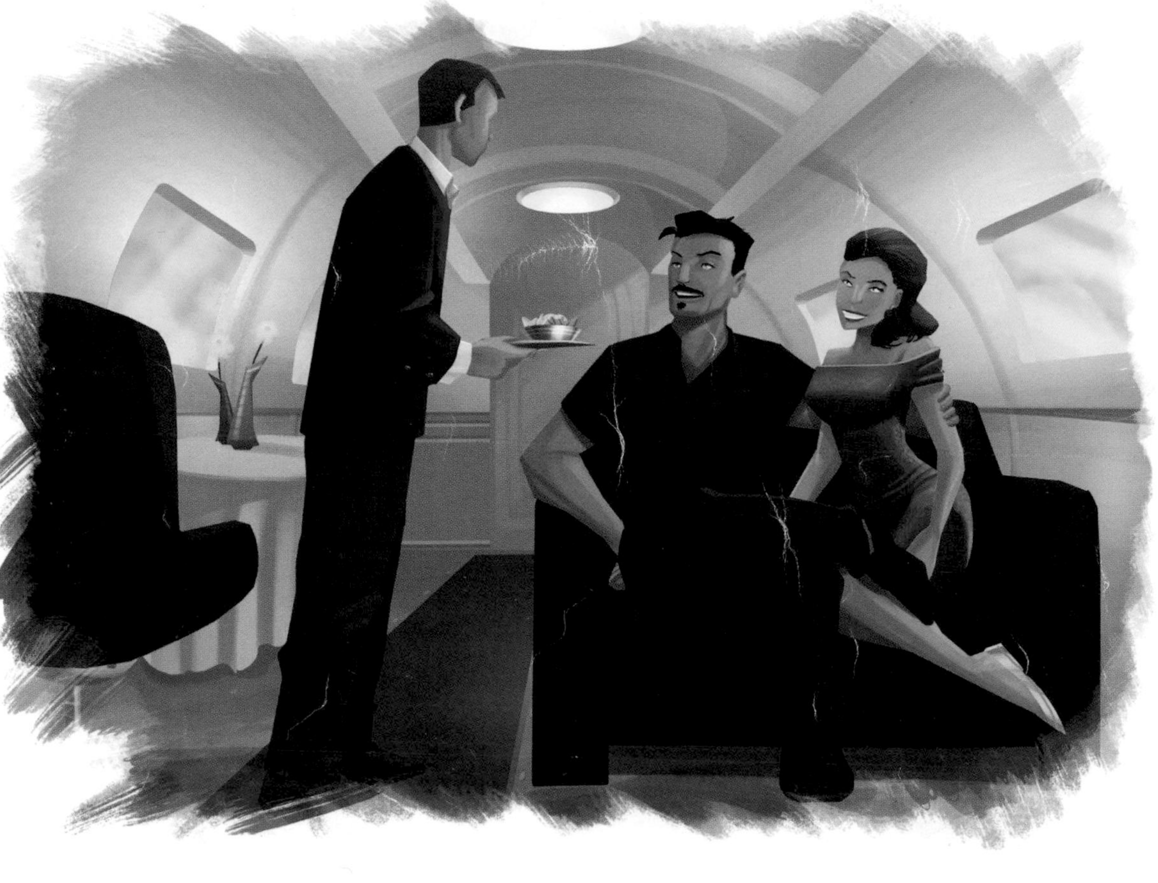

He loved to **have fun.**

And he loved the **finer things** in life.

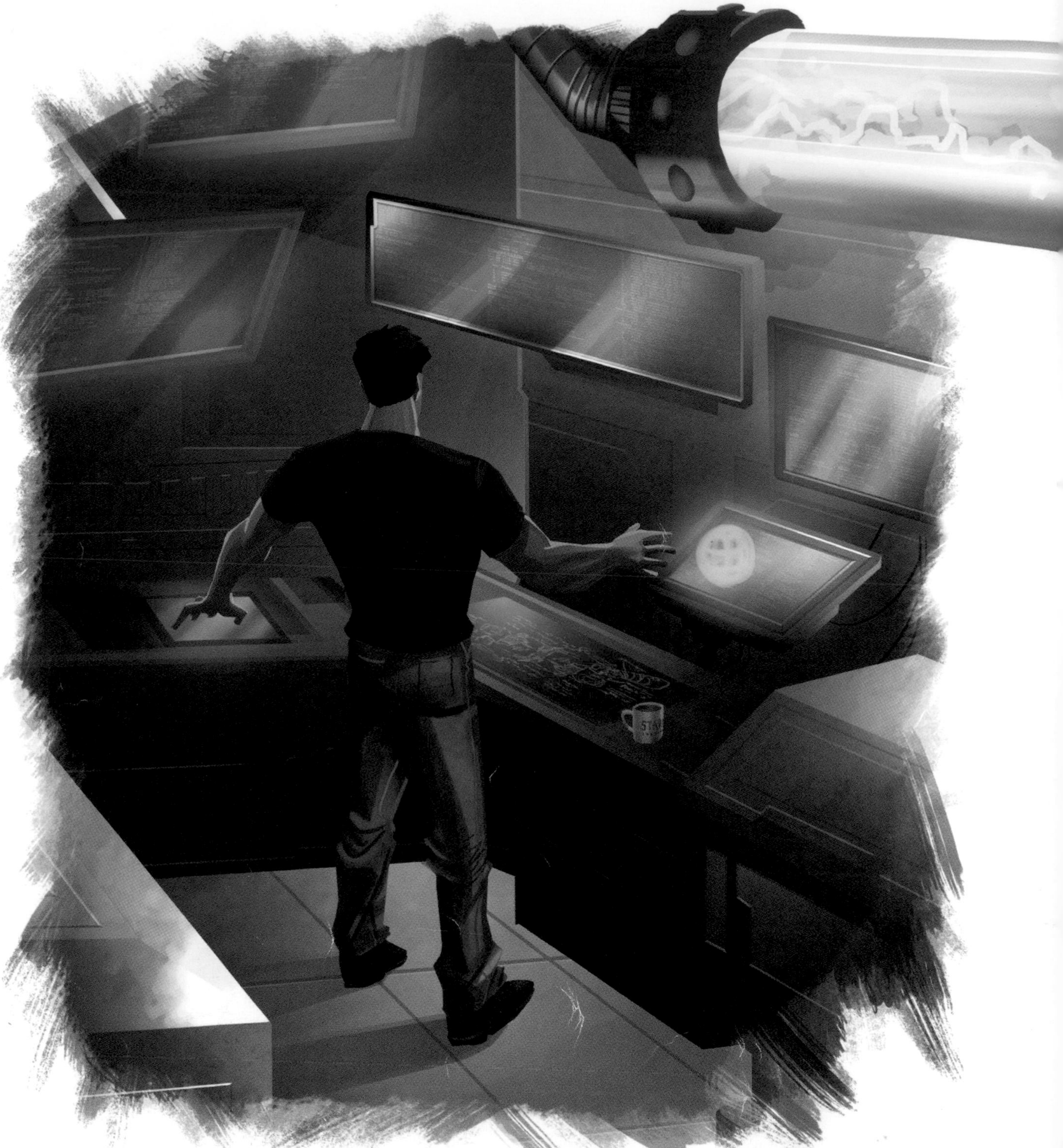

But Tony also worked hard. He was
a **brilliant inventor.** He knew
all sorts of things about **science.**

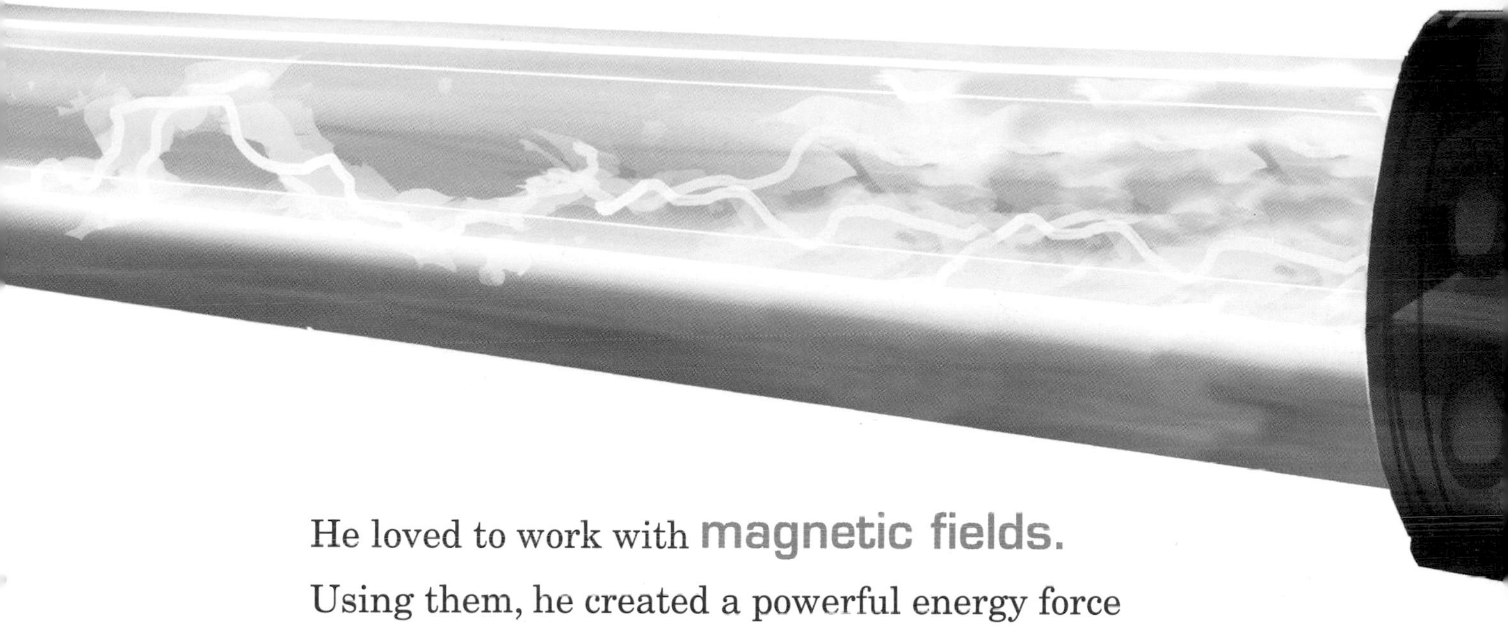

He loved to work with **magnetic fields.** Using them, he created a powerful energy force that he called **repulsor technology.**

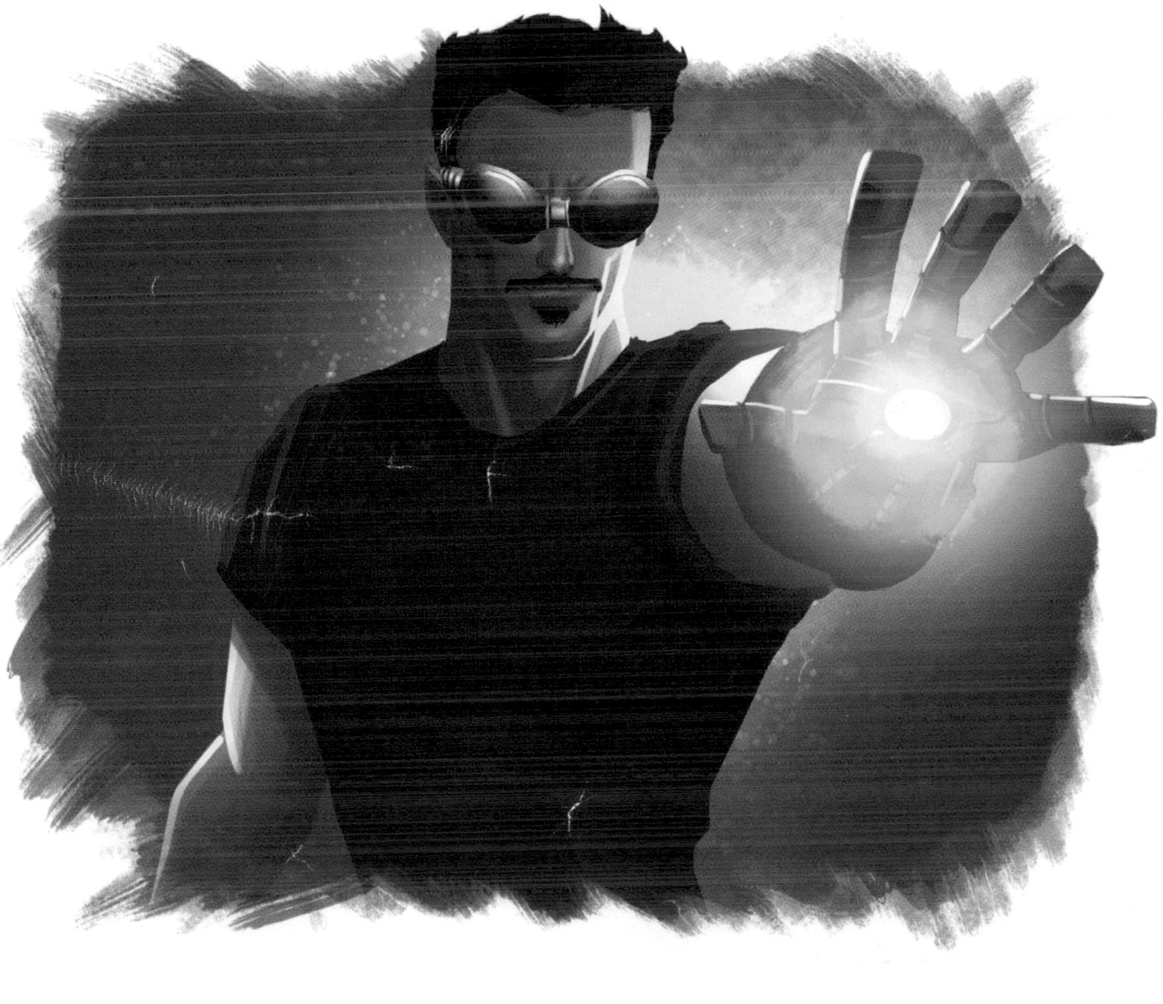

The military was interested in Tony's work. In fact, it was in a **secret Army lab** that Tony's life was forever changed.

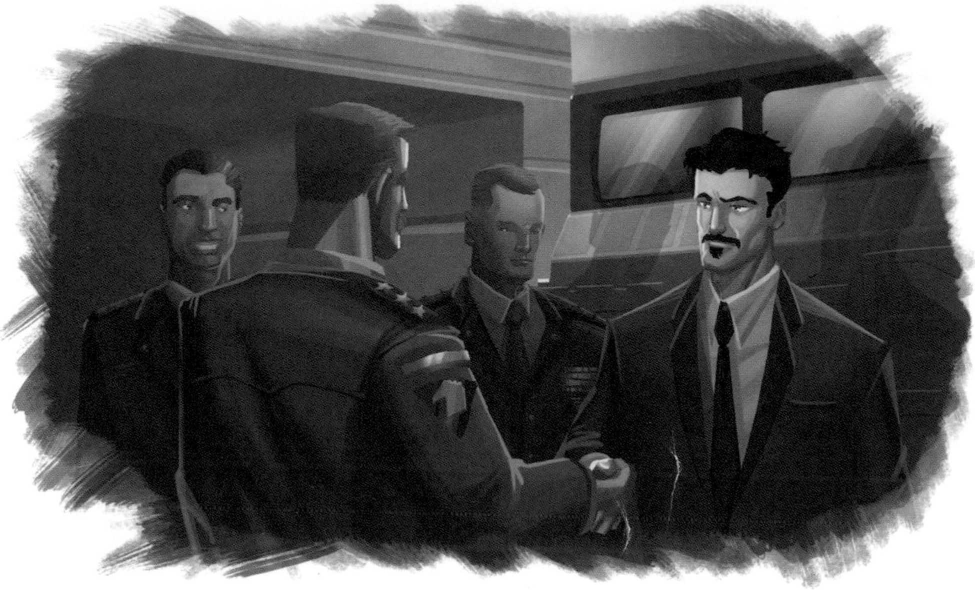

An enemy Army had attacked, and Tony was **badly hurt!**

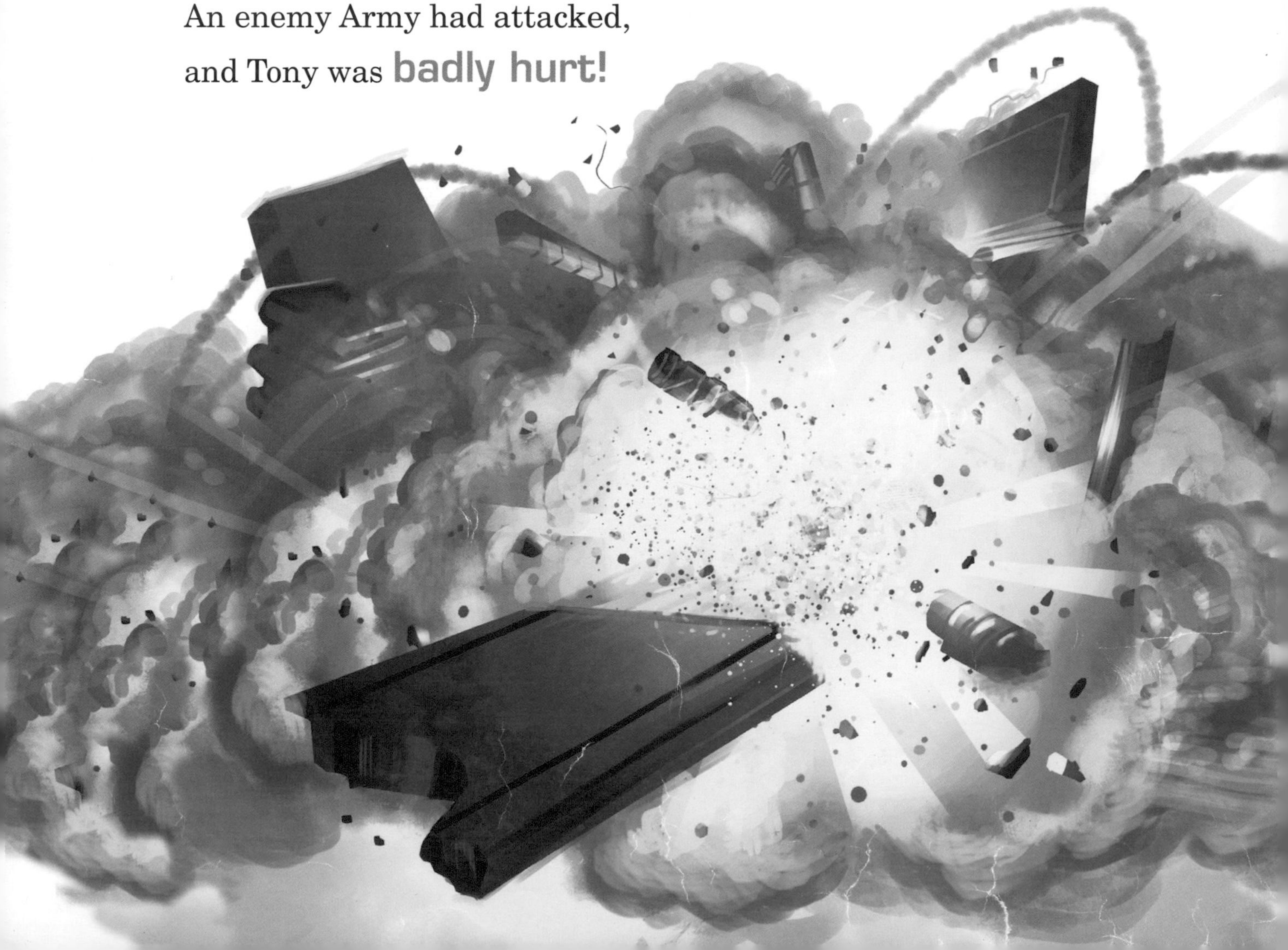

Since, Tony was famous, he was recognized right away.
The enemy knew all about his inventions.

They tossed him in a **prison room** filled with electronic and mechanical equipment. They wanted him to create a mighty weapon for them.

To make things worse, before the enemy left the tiny cell, they told Tony that **his heart had been hurt** in the blast. He did not have much longer to live.

Tony soon found he was not alone in the cell.
The enemy had captured another famous scientist—
PROFESSOR YINSEN.

The enemy wanted the two men to
work together on the great weapon.

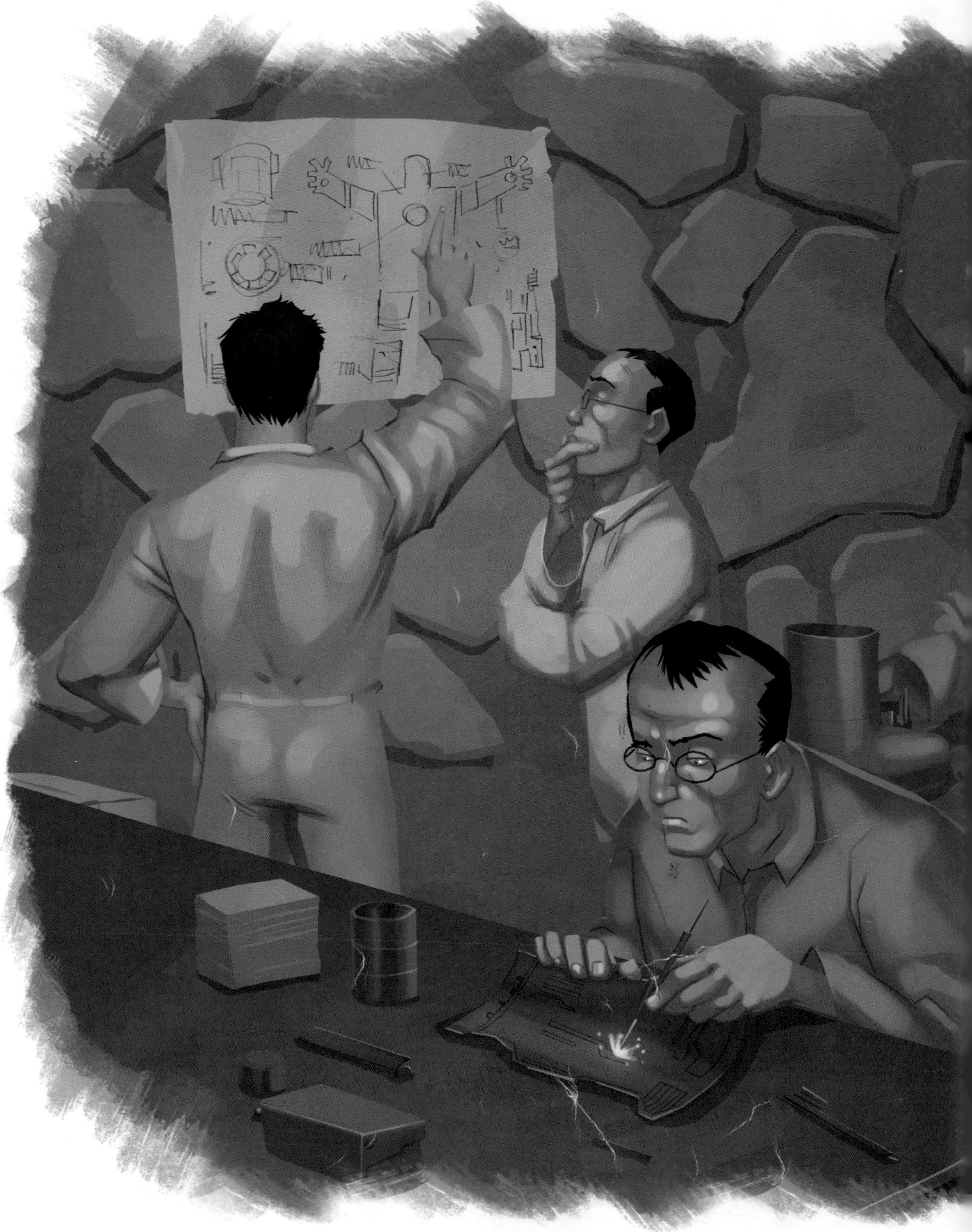

The two men **worked tirelessly** to create something that would save Tony's life. . . .

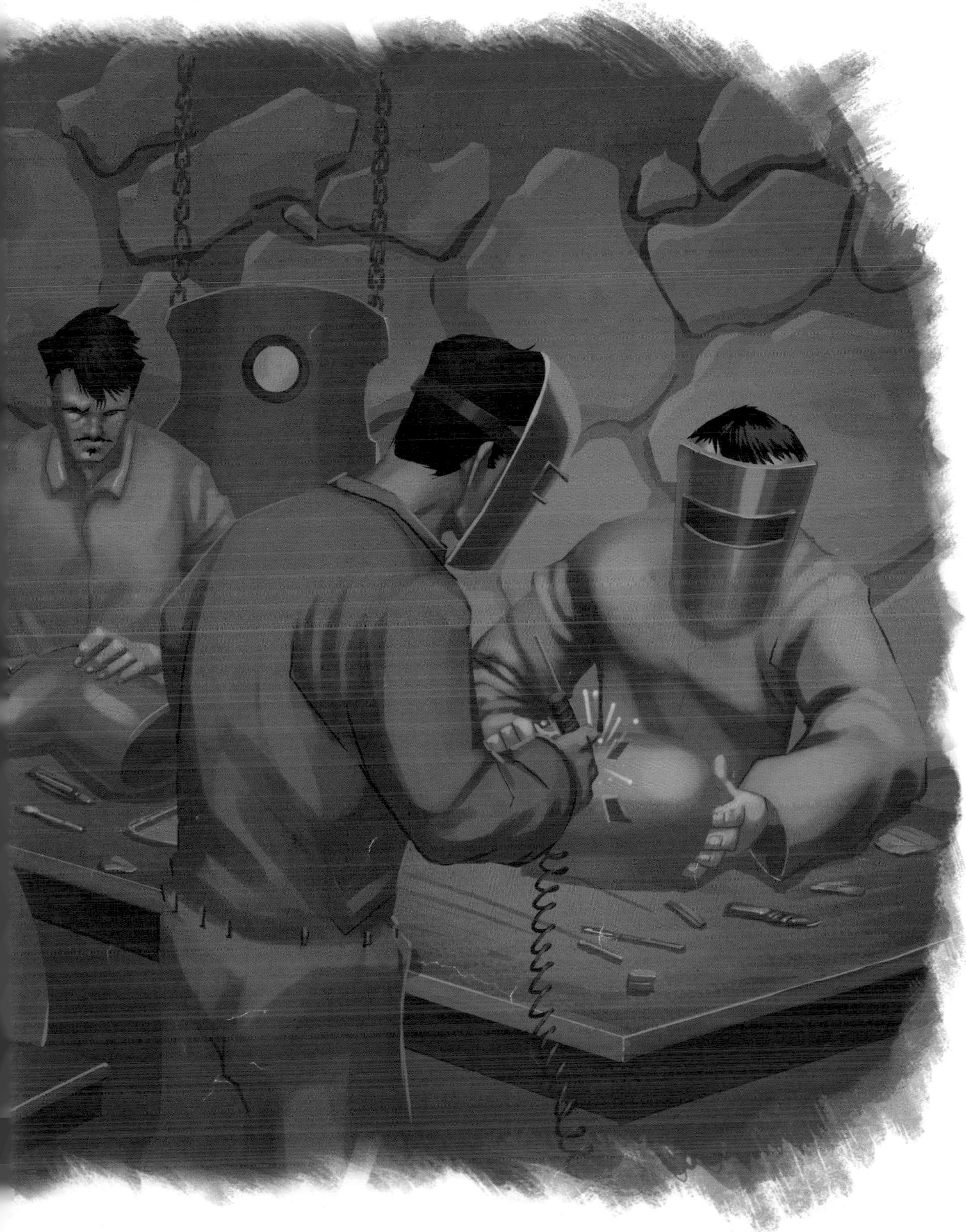

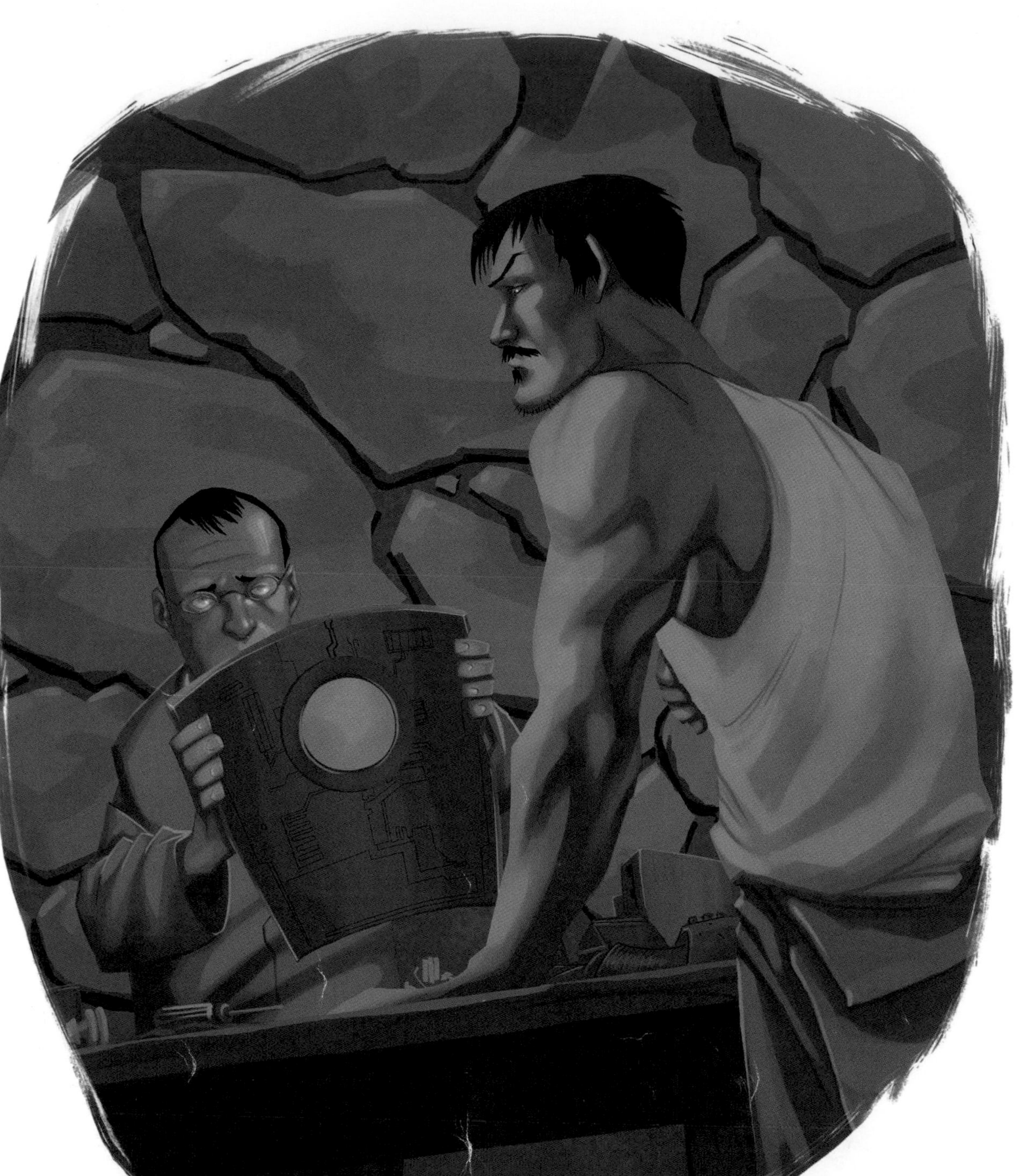

Finally, they **completed the device** that Tony would always need to wear on his chest to keep his heart beating.

But that wasn't **all** they created.

Tony put on the armor . . .

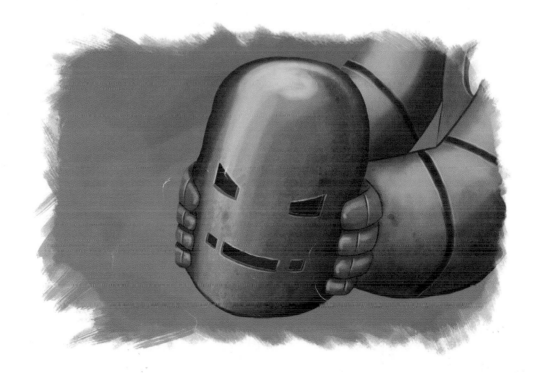

. . . and proved that no walls could hold

the IRON MAN!

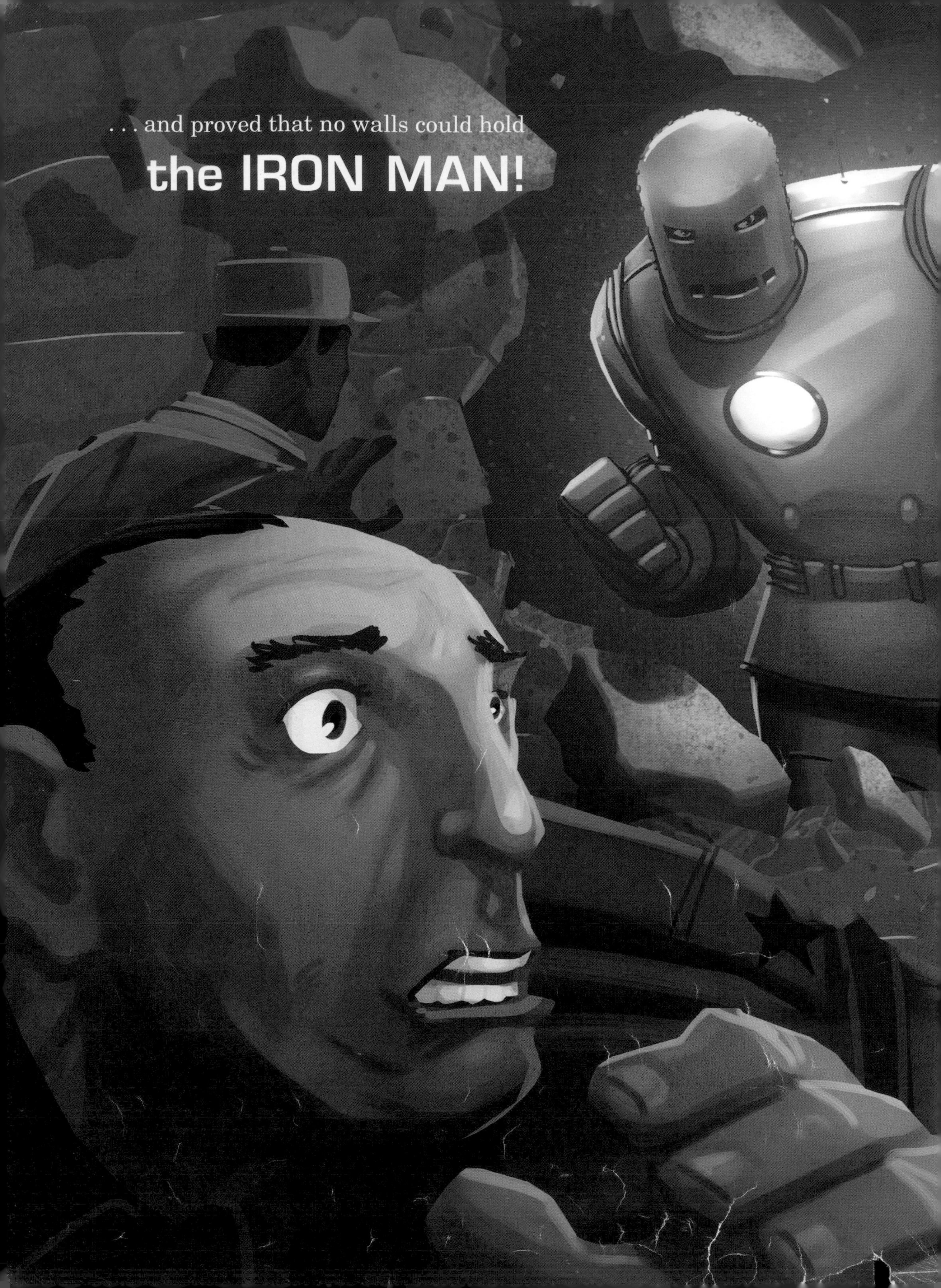

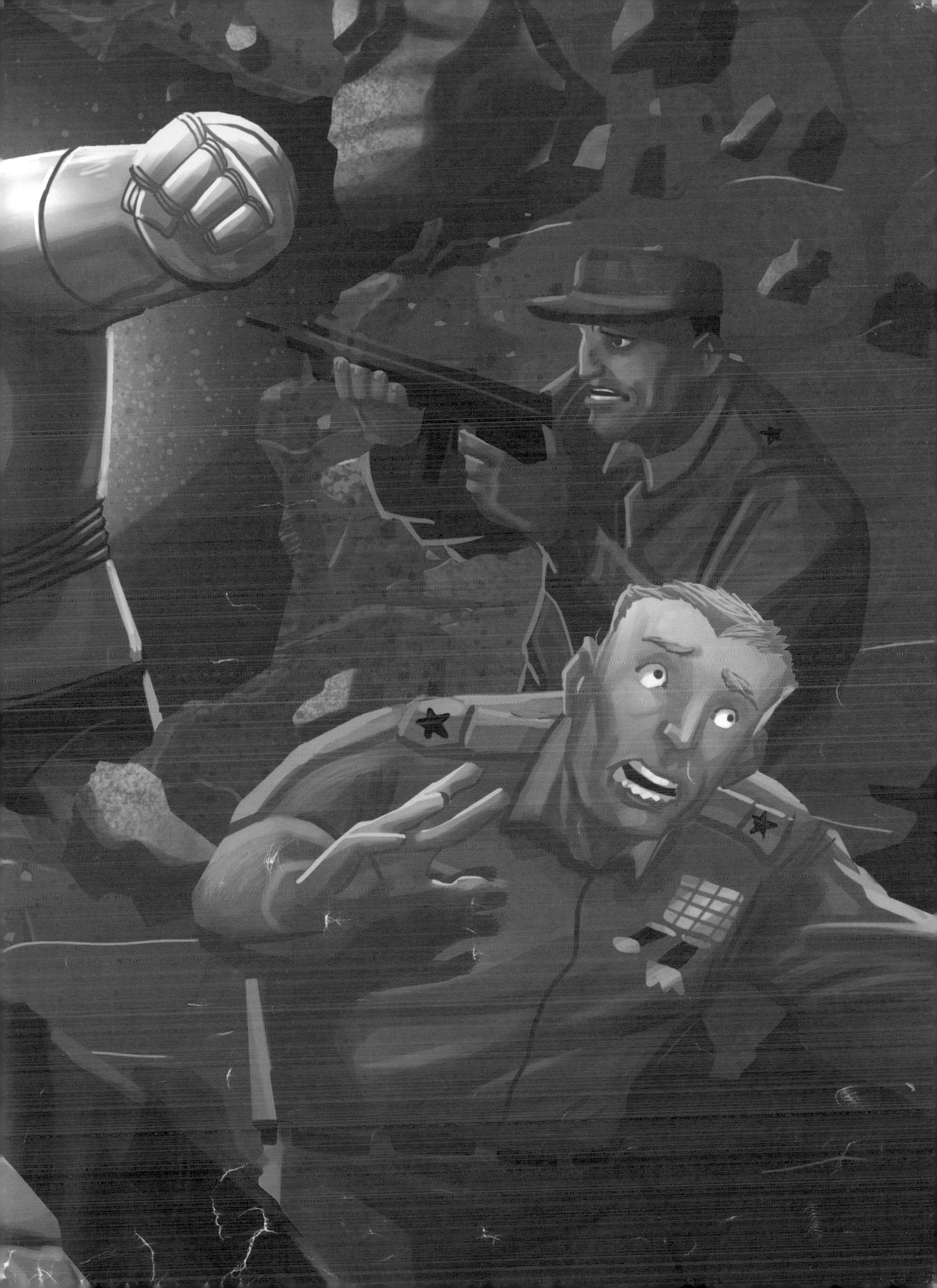

It didn't take long for
the enemy to realize . . .

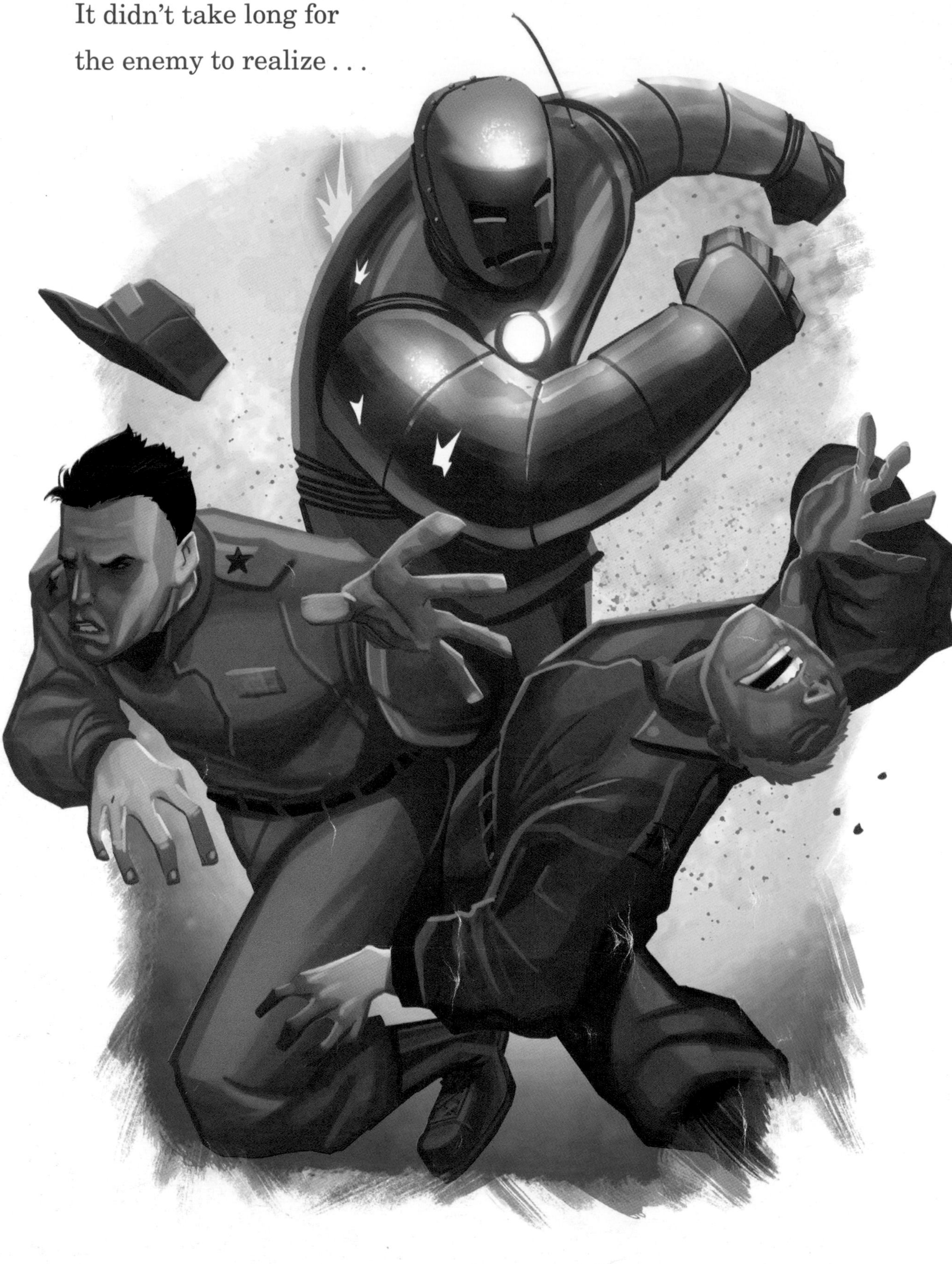

... they were fighting

a losing battle.

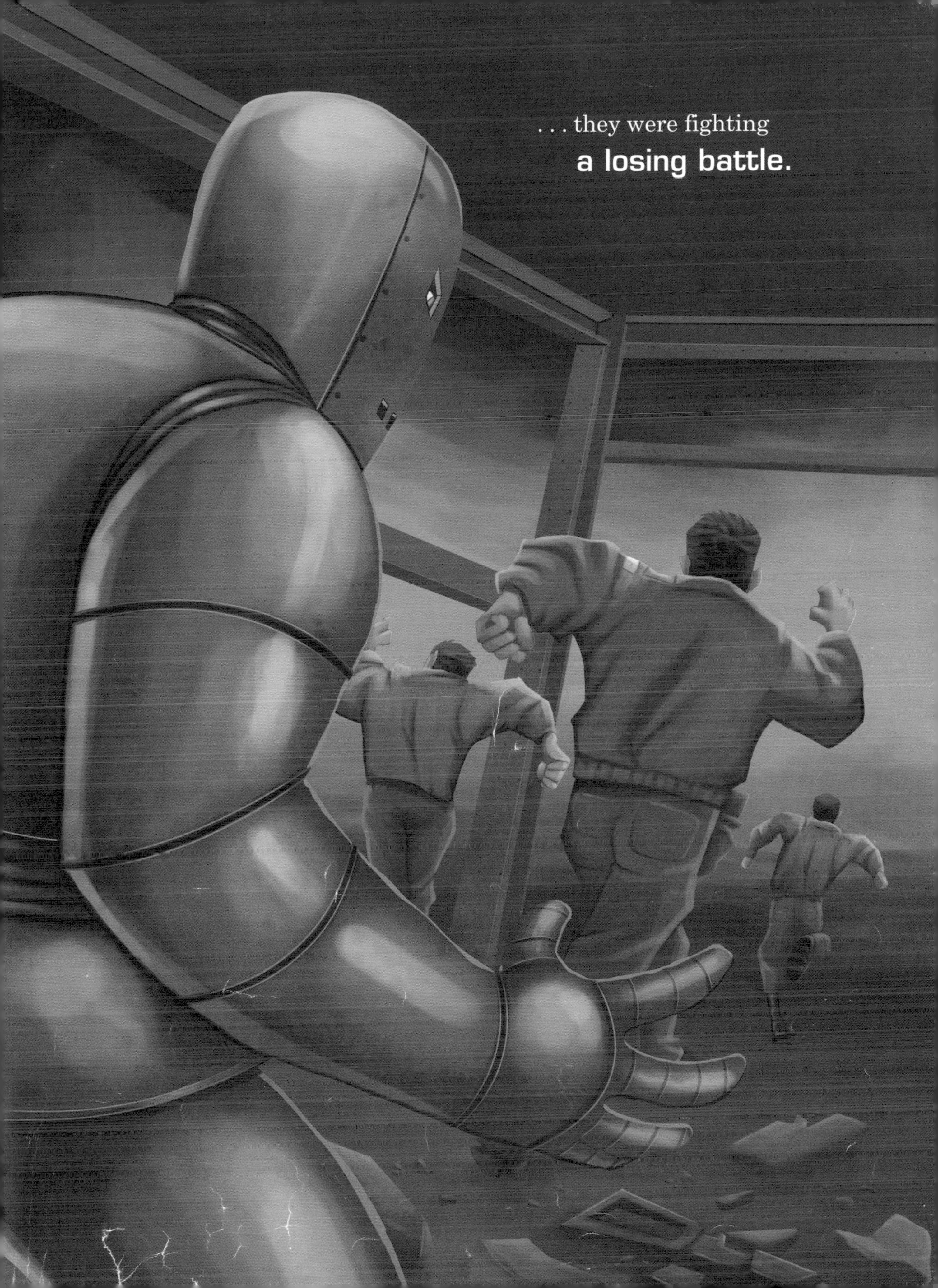

Having **escaped from prison** and saved Professor Yinsen, Tony flew back home.

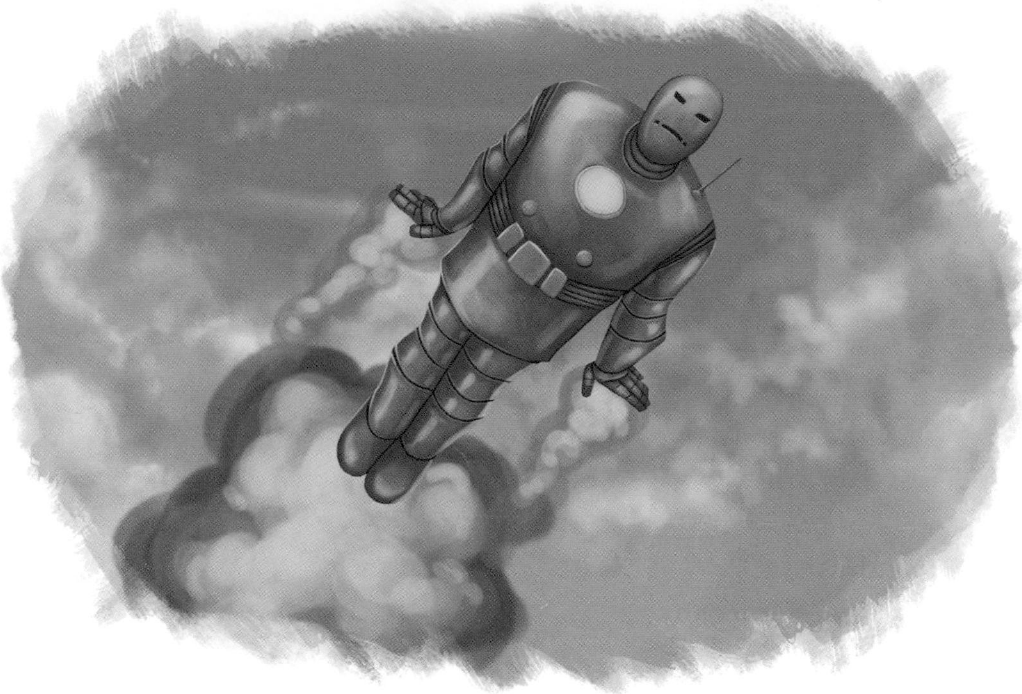

But almost as soon as he got there, he realized that he could now **help** where others couldn't.

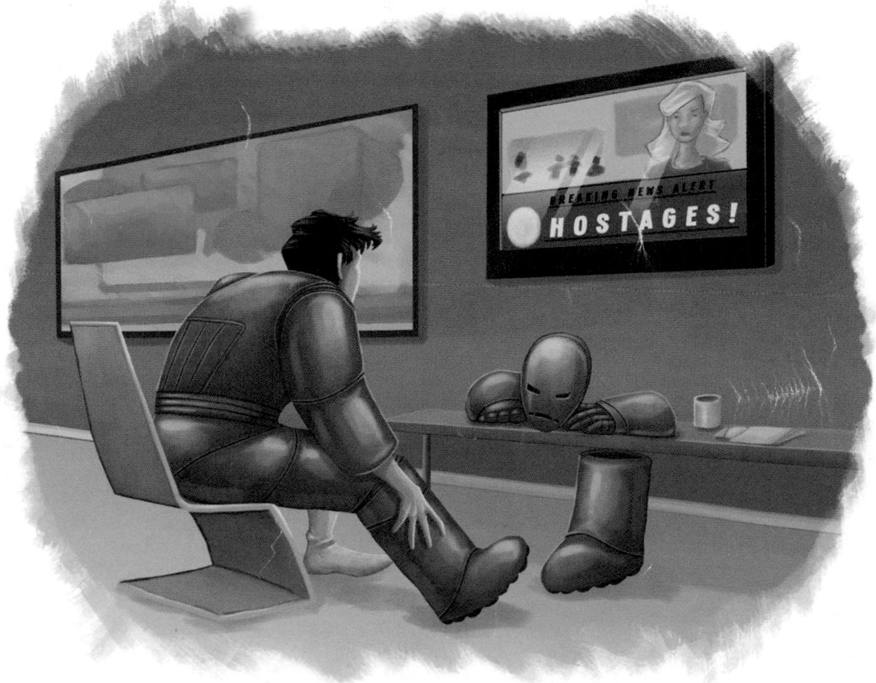
HOSTAGES!

Tony to the rescue!

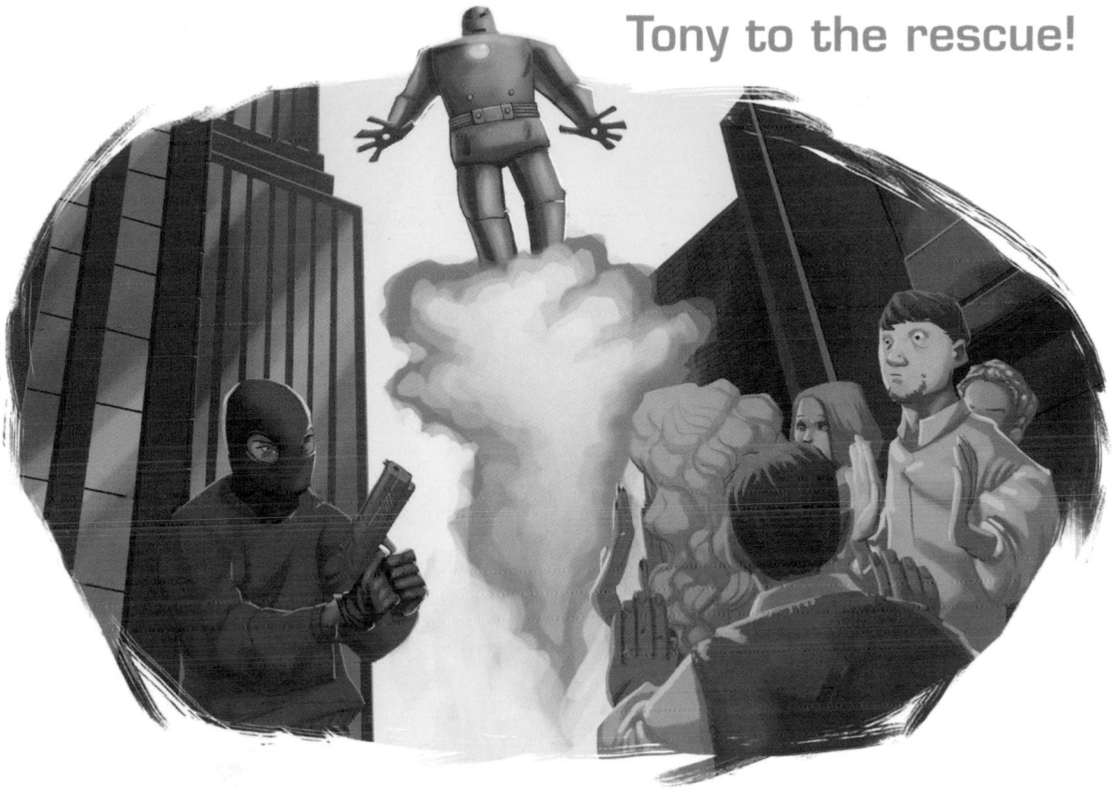

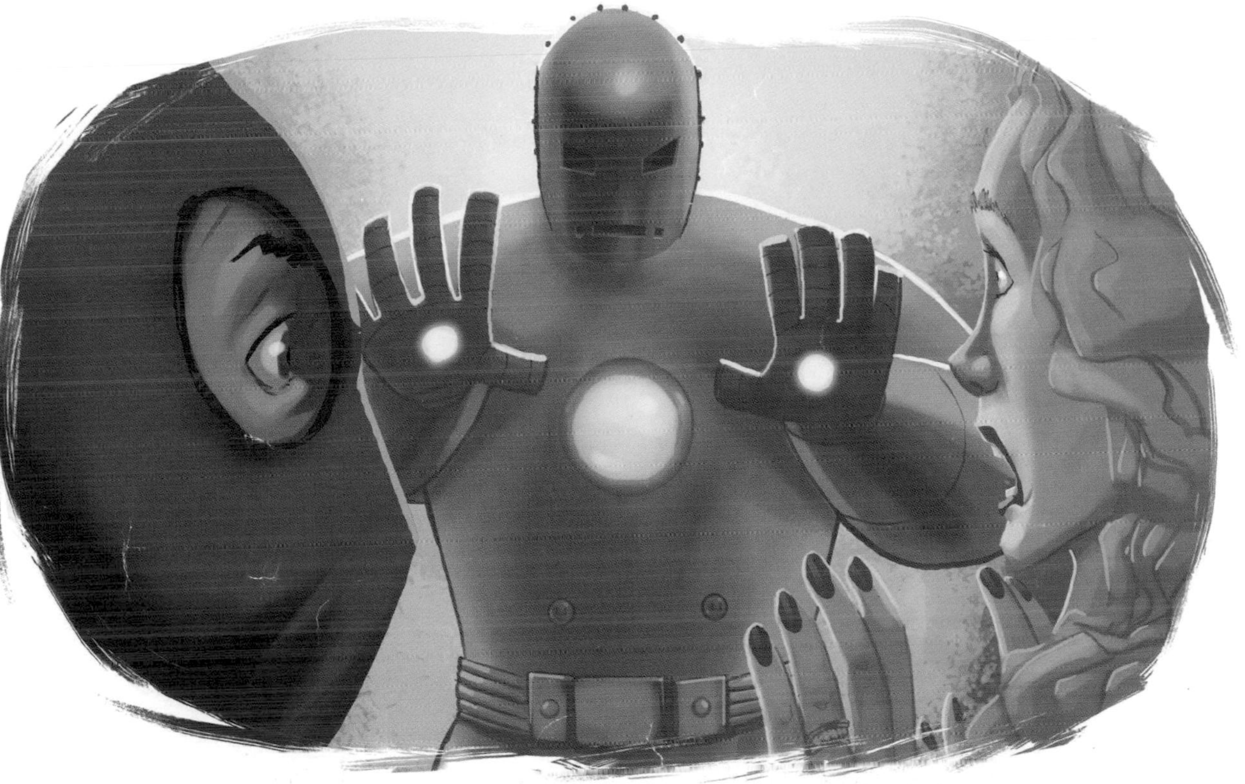

He was strong, unstoppable, **FRIGHTENING!**

Maybe a little **too frightening.**

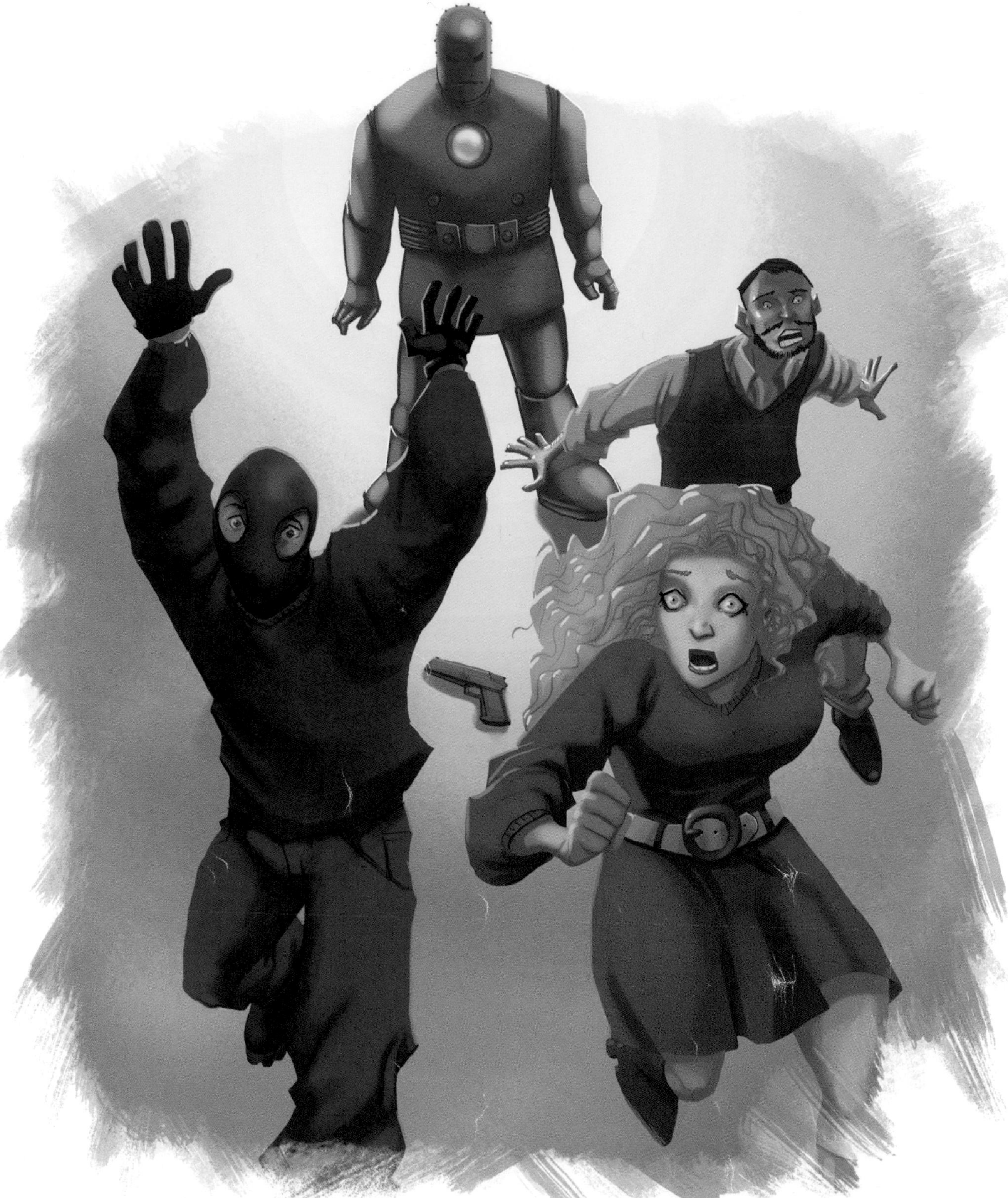

Tony had an **idea.**

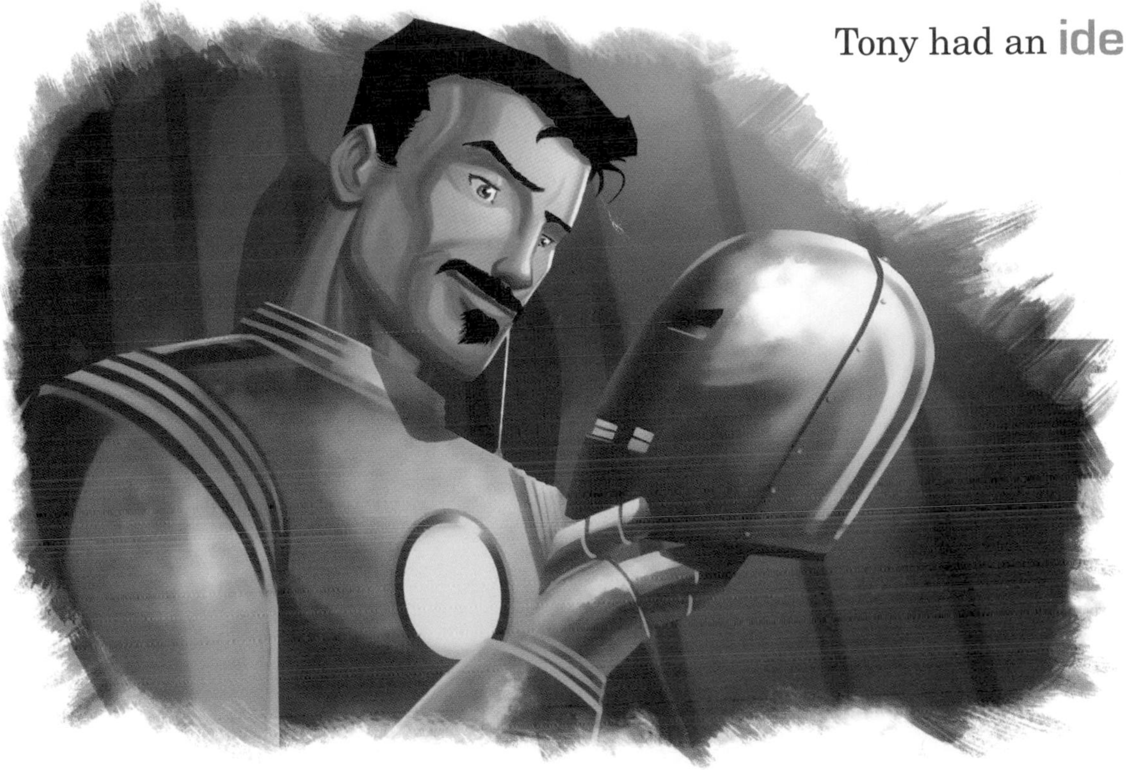

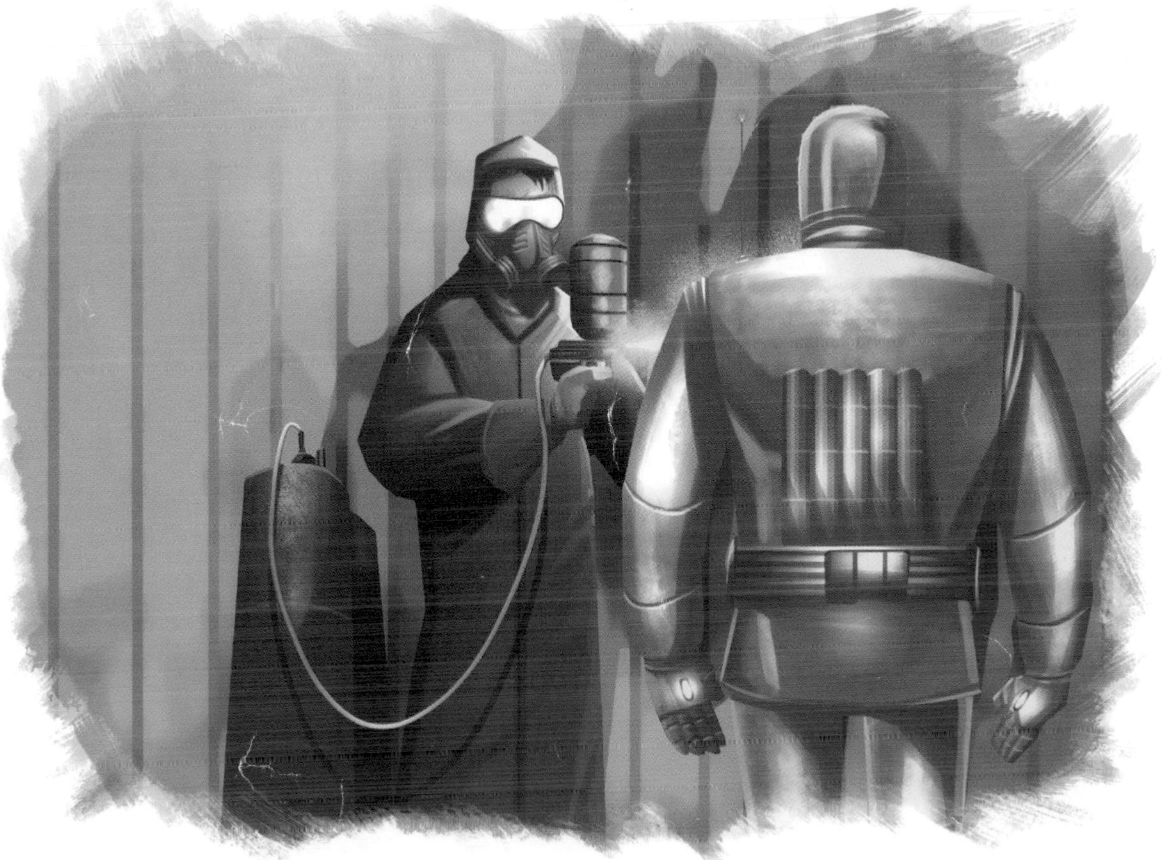

There.

That was better.

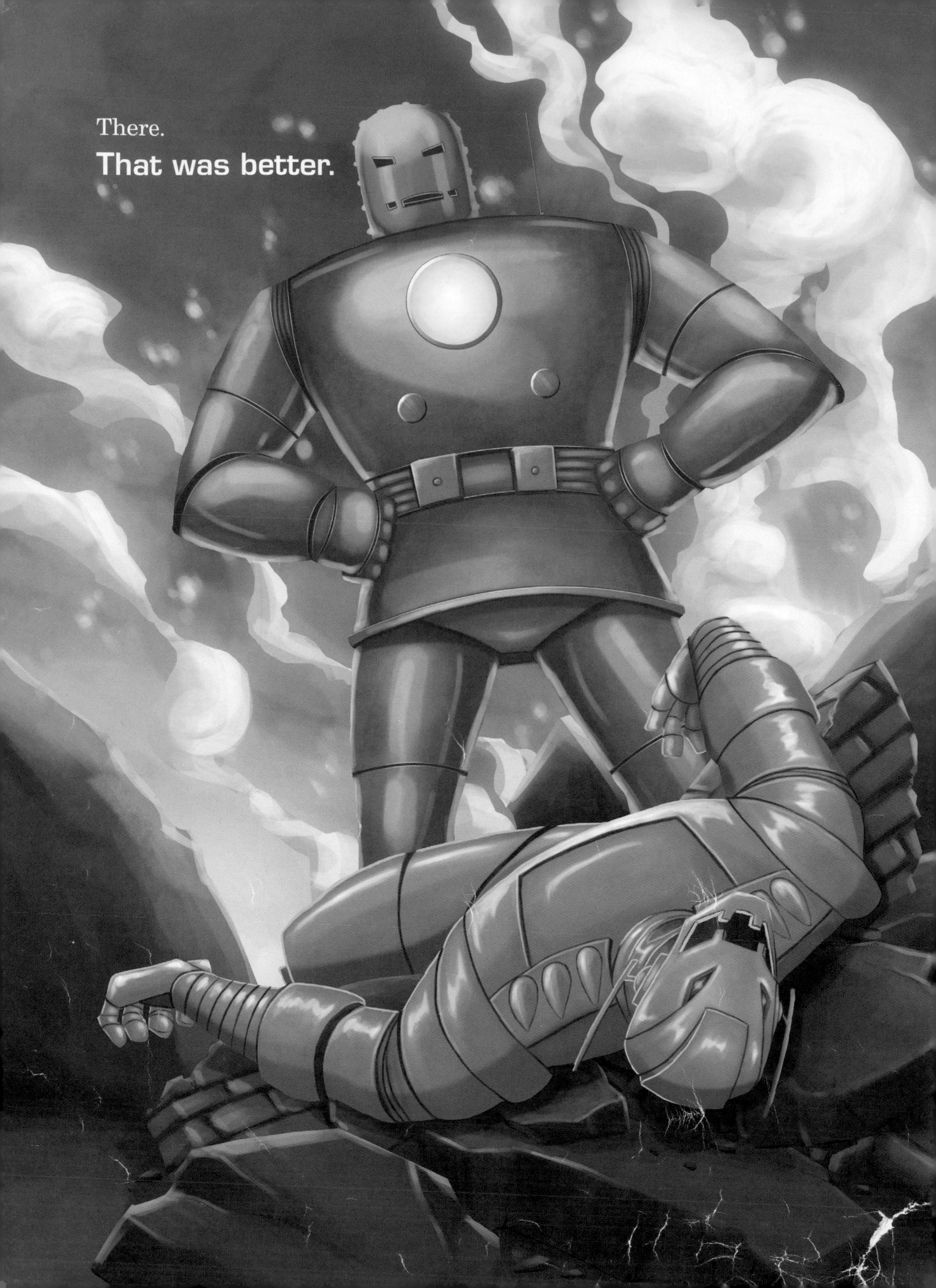

Almost better.

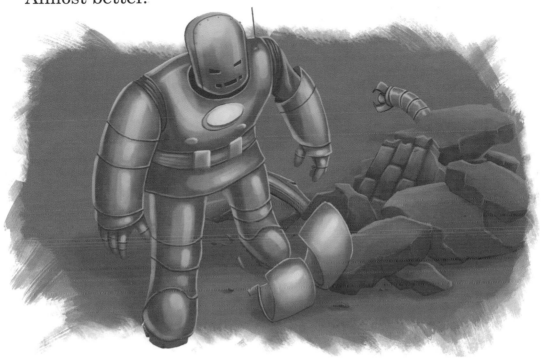

Back to the **drawing board.**

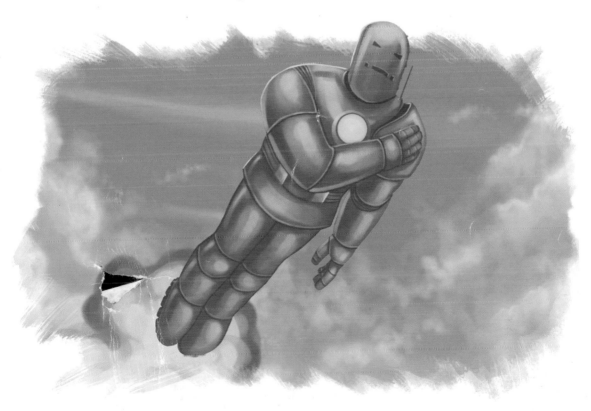

Tony thought that Iron Man needed something as **smooth and stylish** as Tony was.

He needed to create **a lighter suit.**

All he needed was for **his chest plate to remain attached** so his heart would not stop beating.

Everything else could be **changed.**

And a new **Iron Man** was born!

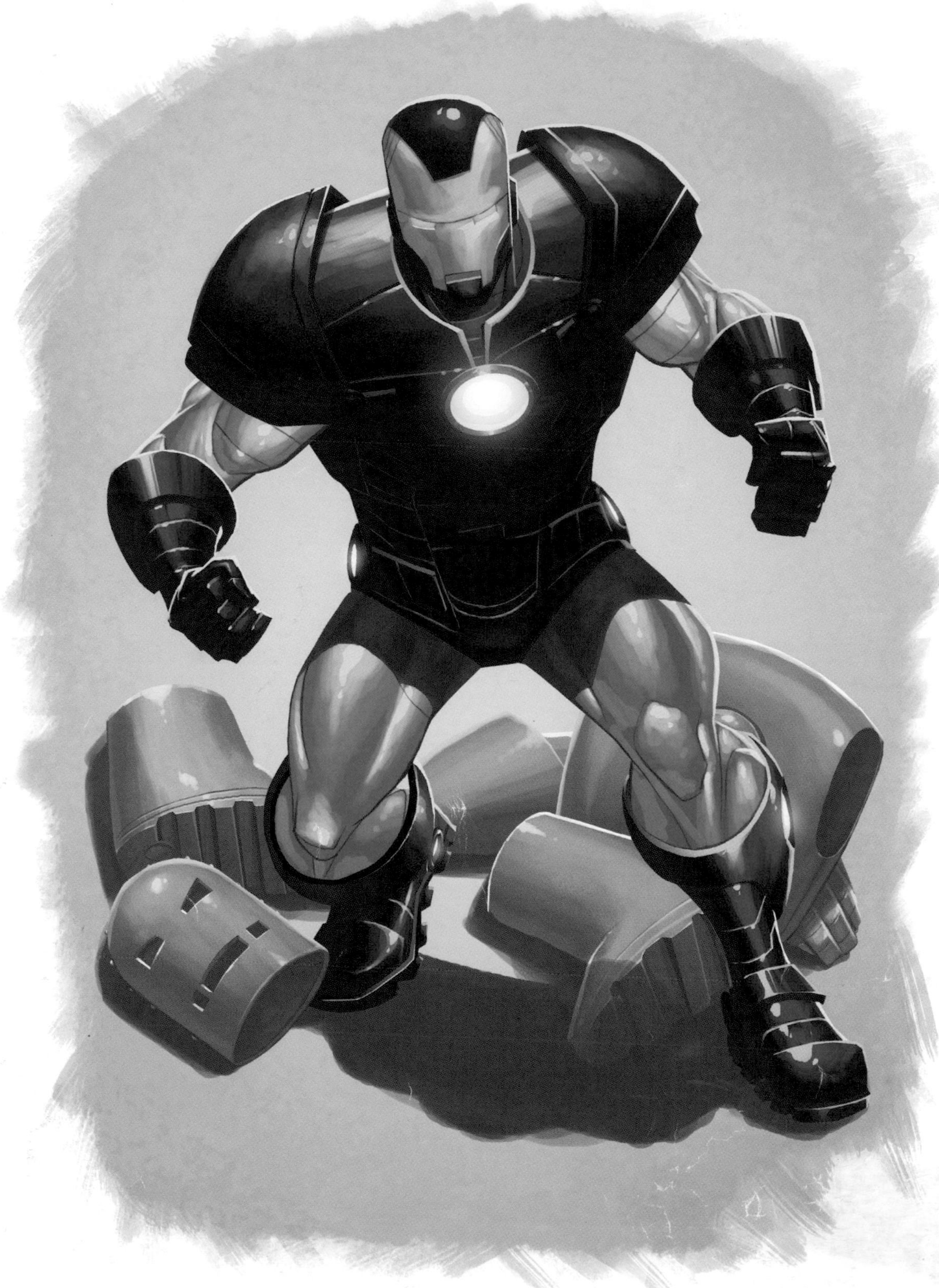

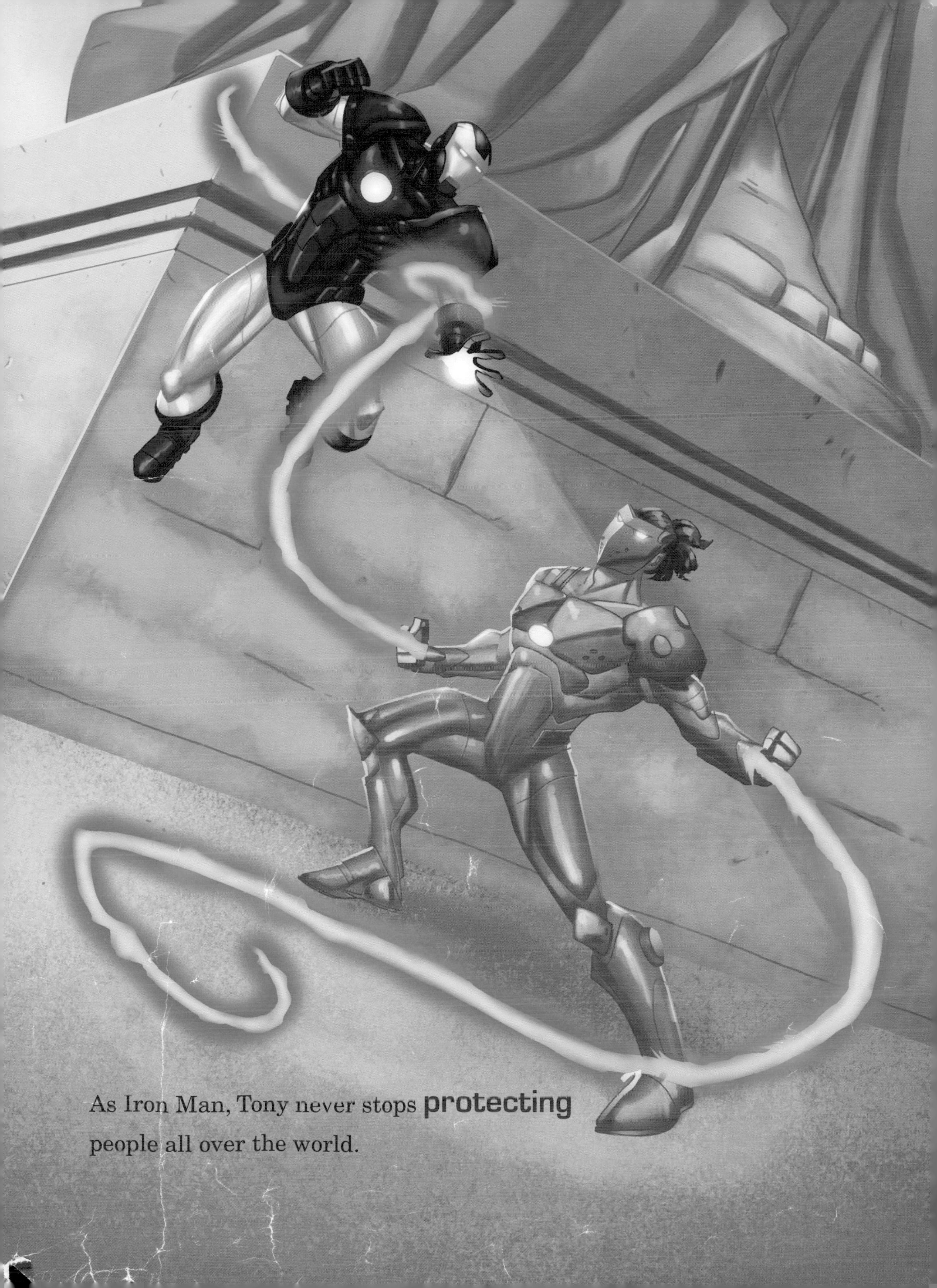

As Iron Man, Tony never stops **protecting** people all over the world.

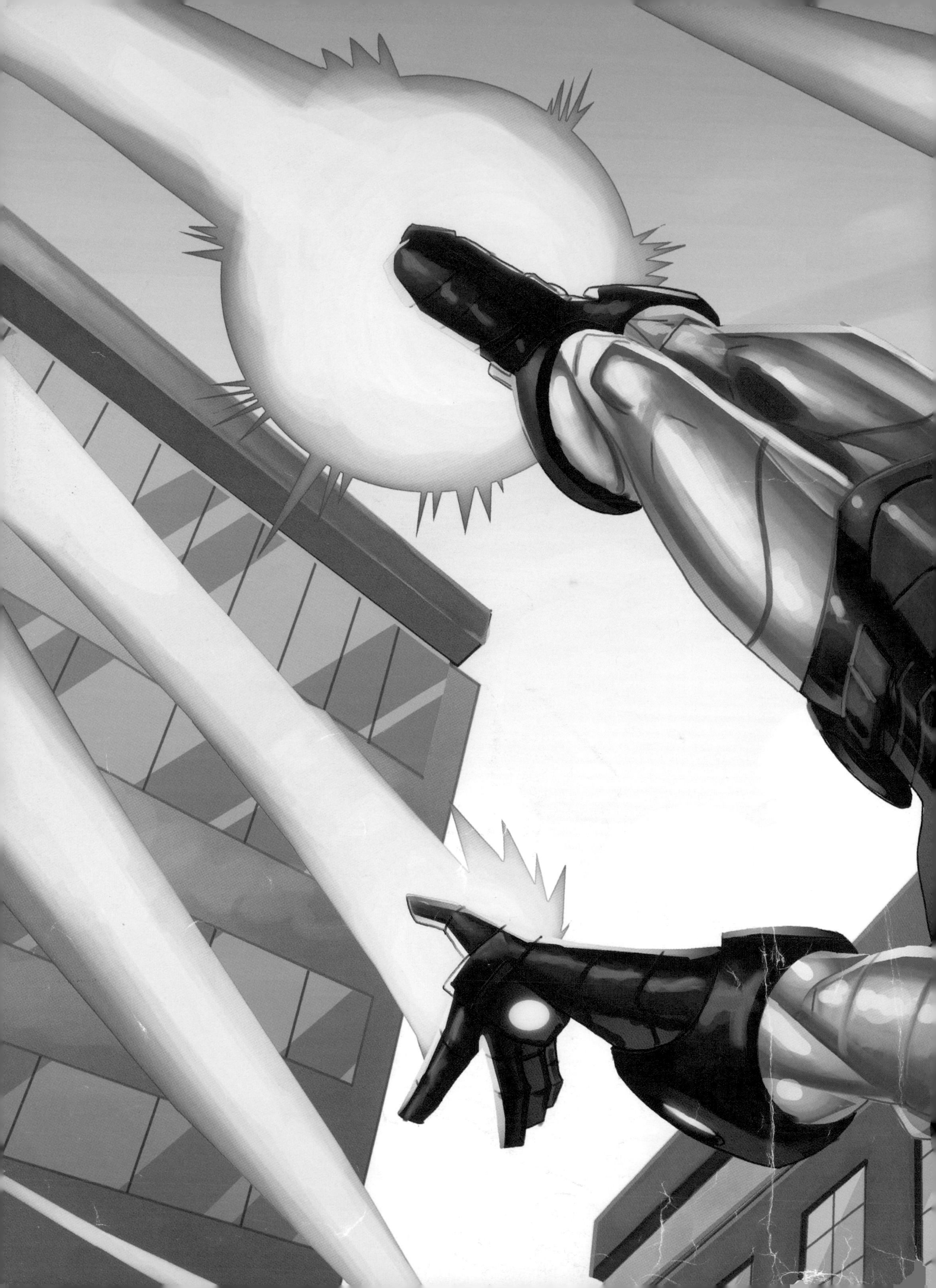

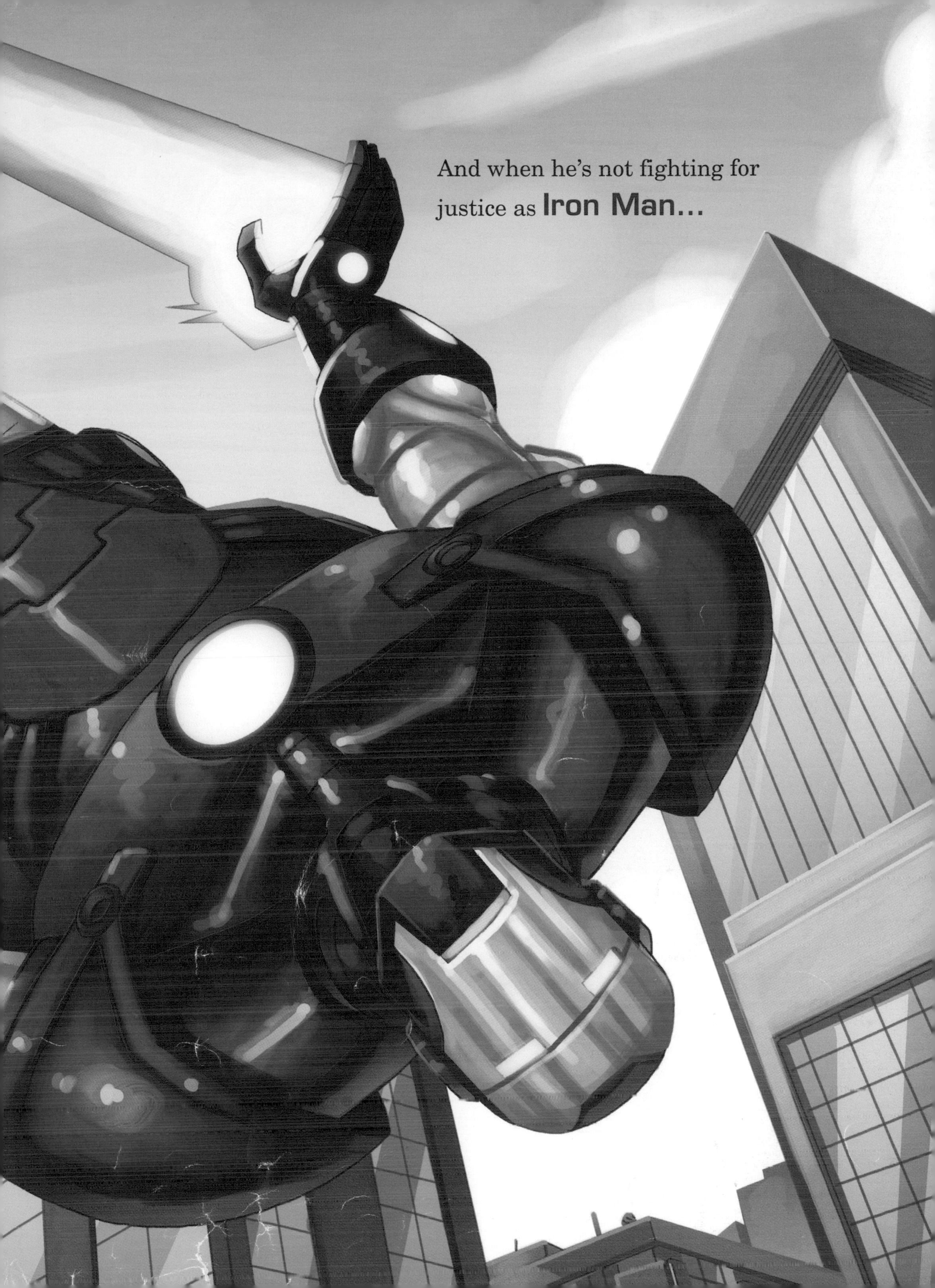

And when he's not fighting for justice as **Iron Man...**

. . . Tony runs his company,

Stark Industries.

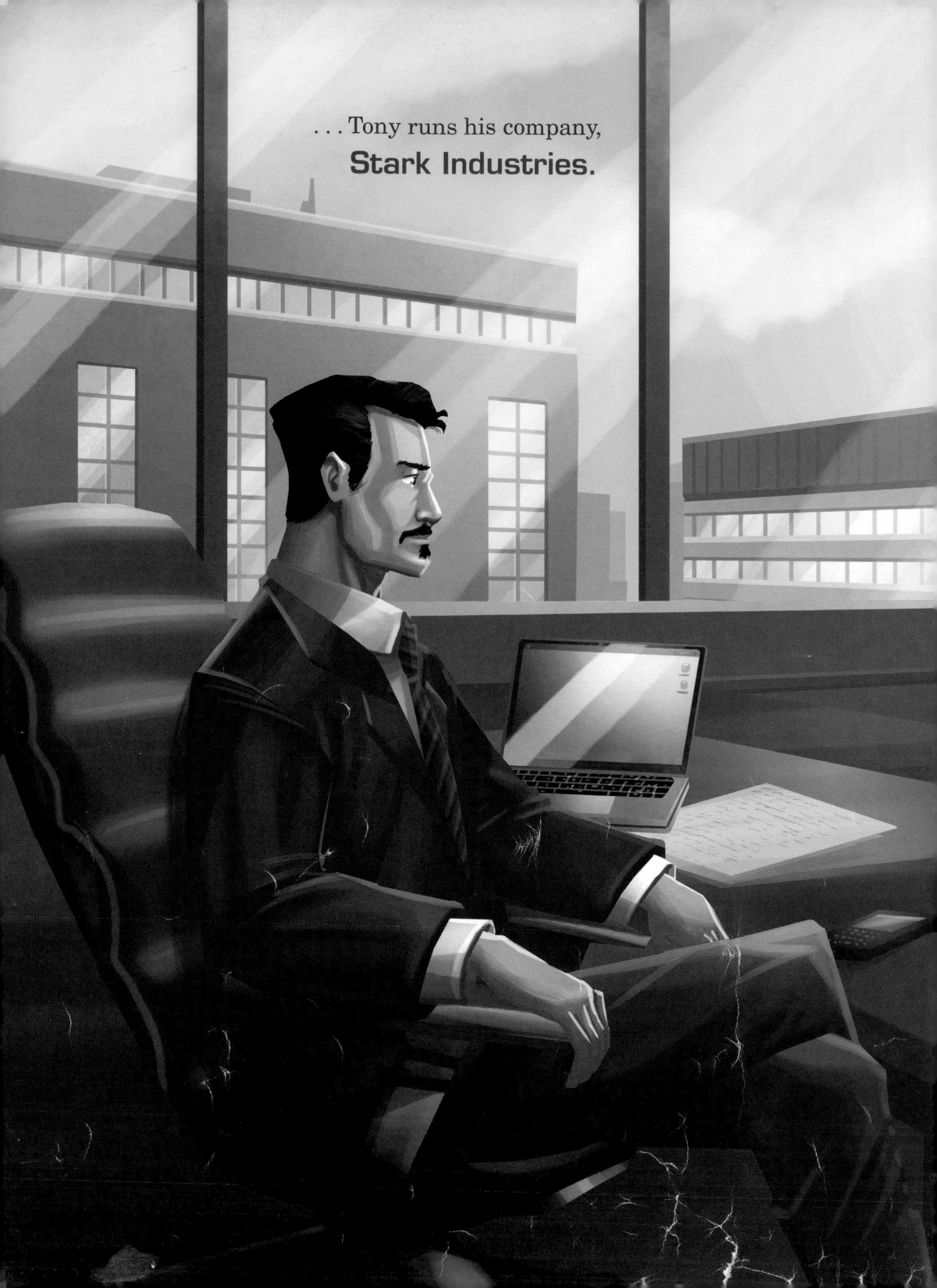

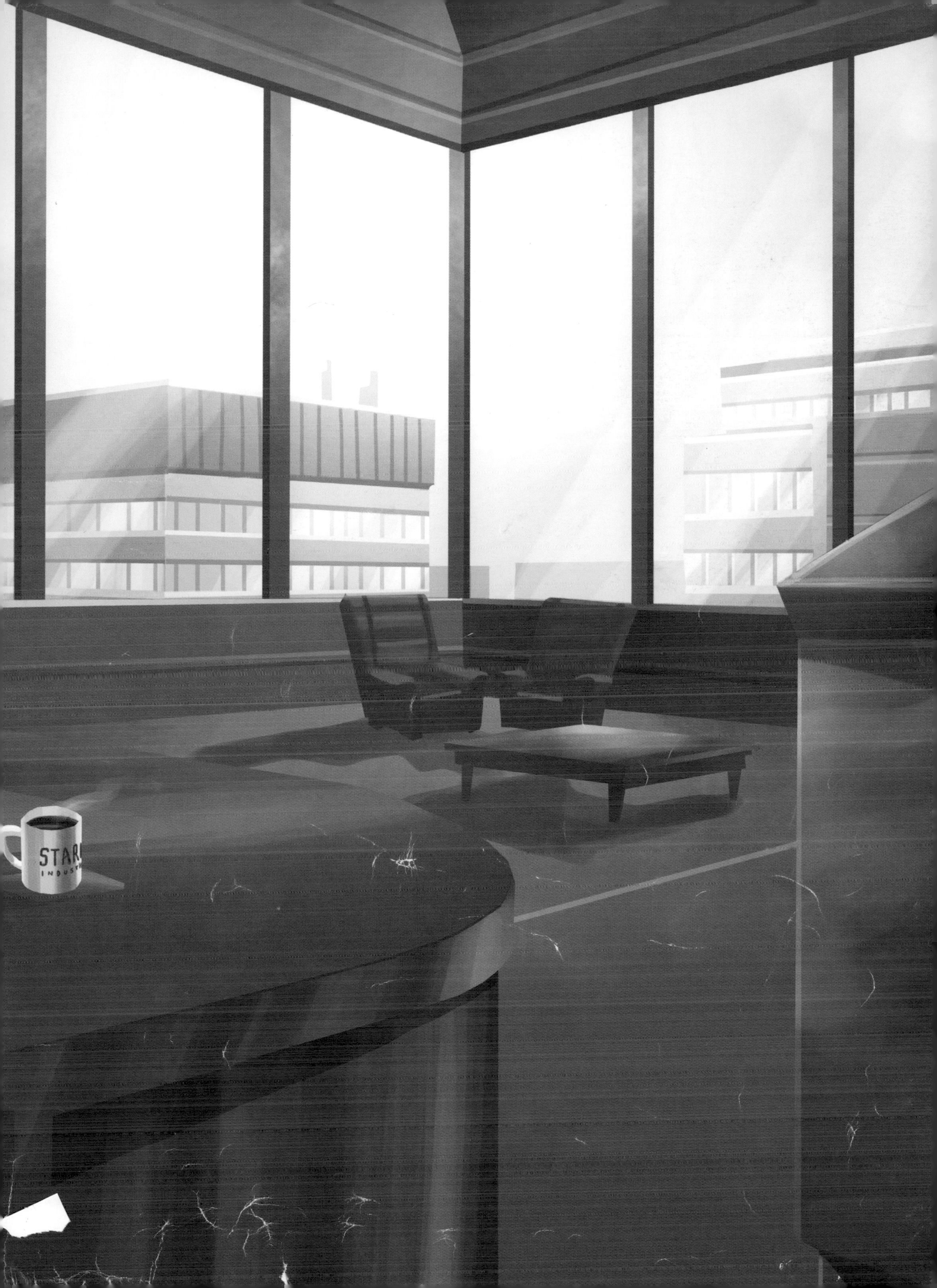

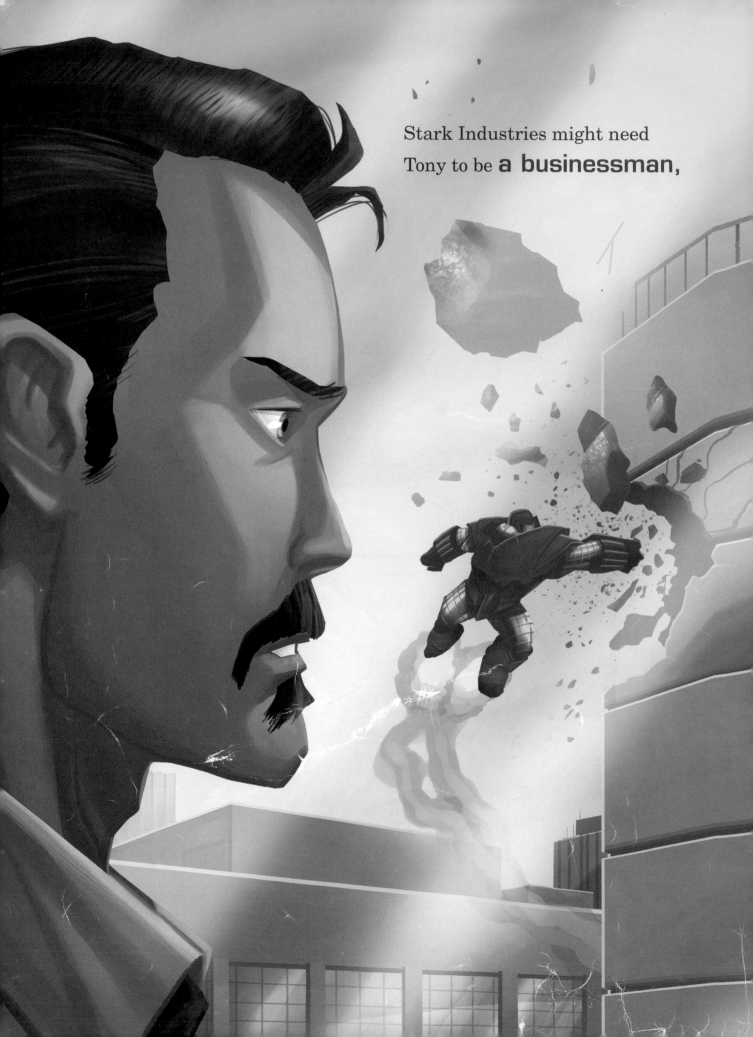

Stark Industries might need Tony to be **a businessman,**

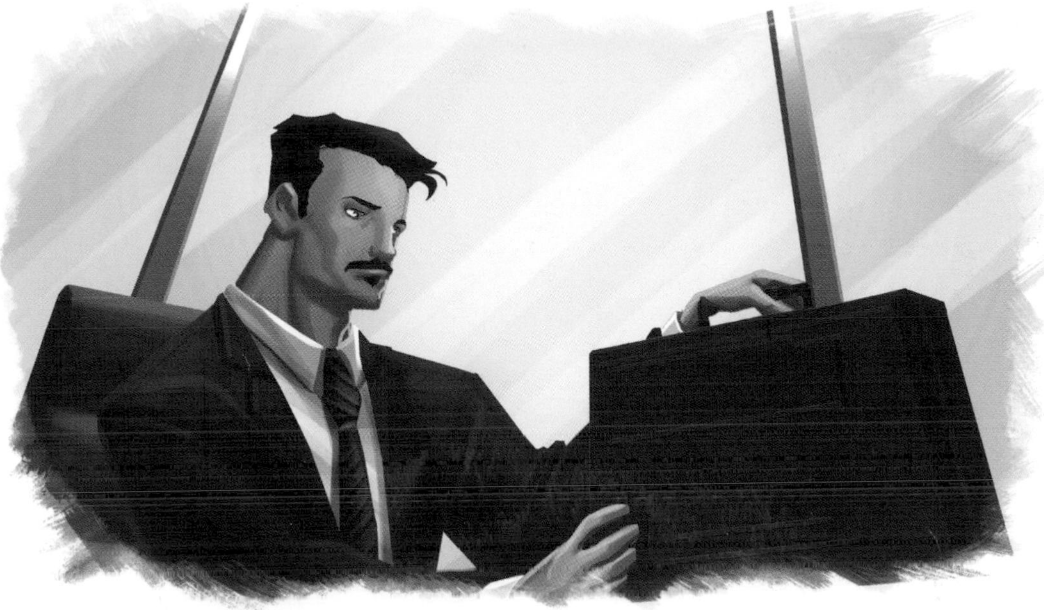

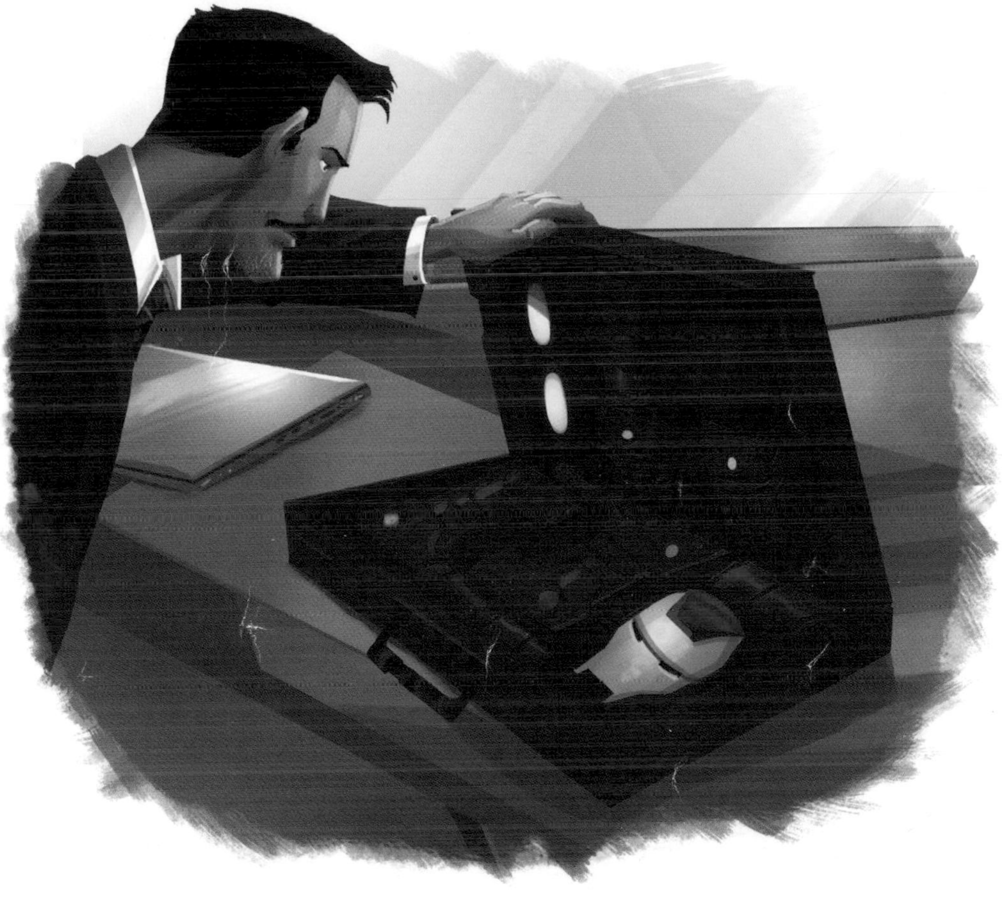

but with new villains attacking every
day, the world needs Tony to be

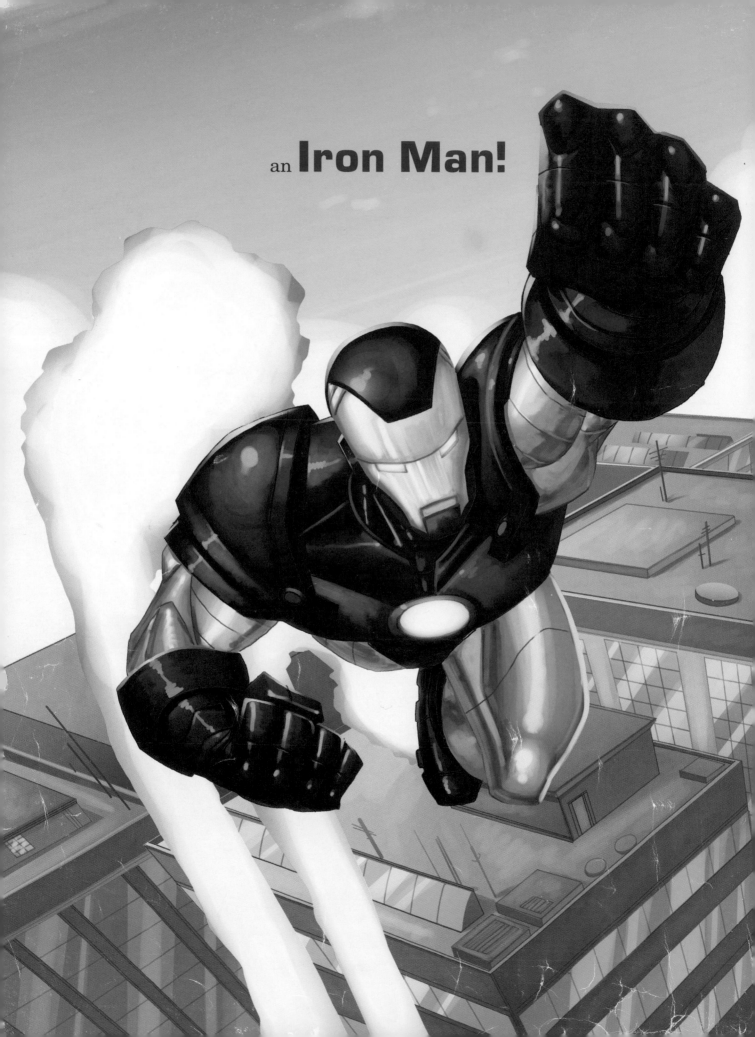

an **Iron Man!**

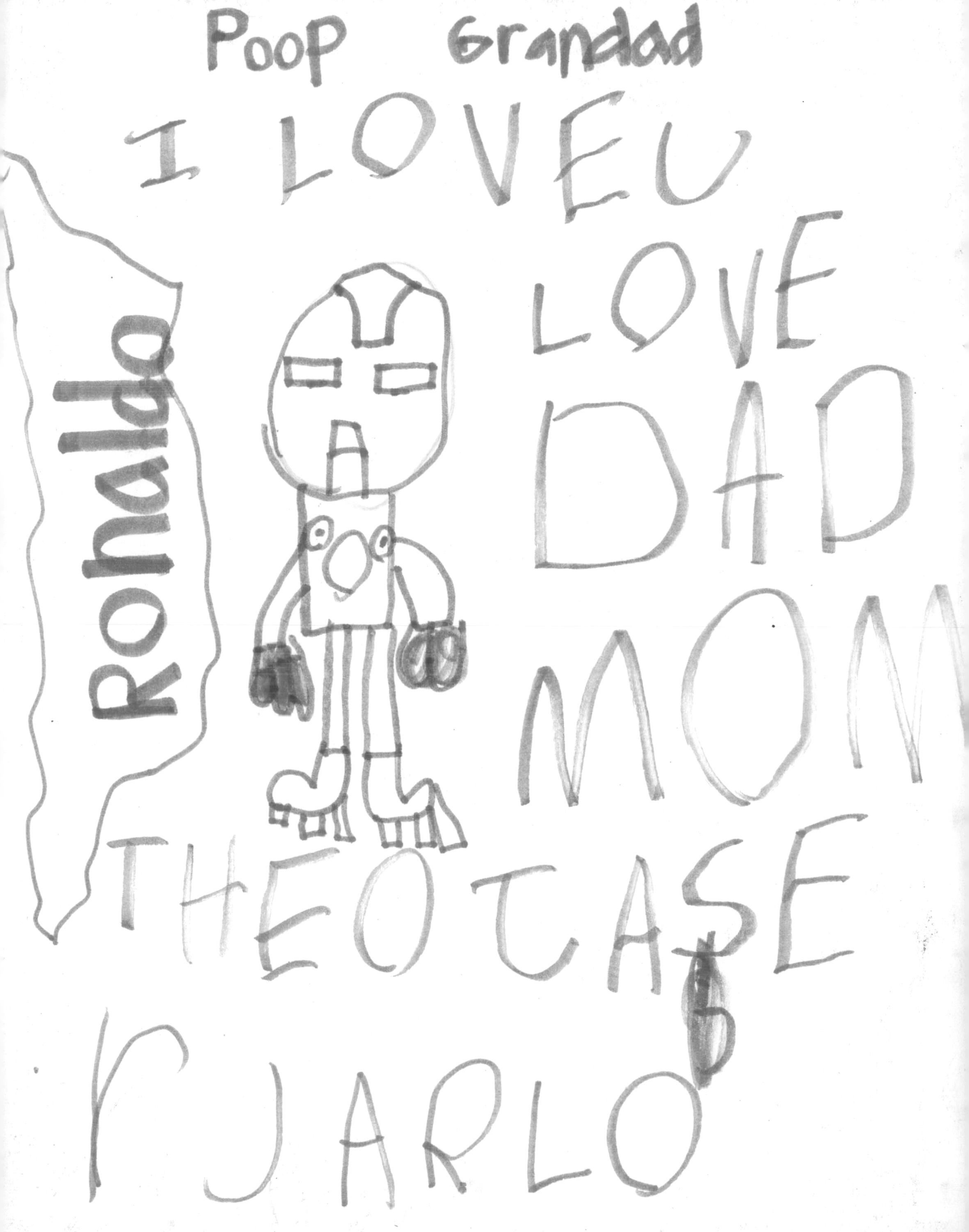

Poop Grandad
I LOVE U
LOVE
DAD
MOM
THEO CASE
rJARLO
Ronaldo